A BEGINNING

and other stories

by

WALTER
DE LA MARE

FABER AND FABER
24 Russell Square
London

First published in mcmlv
by Faber and Faber Limited
24 Russell Square London W.C.1
Second impression November mcmlv
Printed in Great Britain by
Latimer Trend & Co Ltd Plymouth

CONTENTS

INTRODUCTION

In "advanced years", I fancy, one's lifelong frailties may appear (if only to oneself) to be easily excused and possibly even amusing. In this minor degree we become philosophers. And yet—it is not easy either to condone or explain how a practised writer can bring himself to making notes, for a short story, let us say, in a handwriting he will only with extreme difficulty, or, perhaps, never, be able to read; and in terms in which he may fail to find either sense or significance. Until, that is, he realizes that his scribble was not intended to be the outline of a plot but to recall an emotion, a state of being, a sense of the strange, a dream on the borderline, an atmosphere.

This, alas, has been my practice and experience for years and years. Stories, in any case, are strange phenomena, and may (when legible) seemingly stay alive as long as their writer is destined to do. They may in this process pass through a hibernation more protracted than any bear or butterfly is likely to survive, and may then come alive again. Even in hibernation they are not always sleeping. Moreover, the *conception* of a story (as perhaps that of ourselves) is probably of more significance than its gestation.

All fiction indeed, in its conception, seems to follow in essence a life of its own, and one perhaps of unexpected vicissitudes. And afterwards? Wasn't it over Balzac's stories, when in proof, that his printers nearly lost their reason? As for fiction's silent imagery —life, I remember being told on good authority that, when Henry James was on his deathbed, he still had a number of novels—novels-to-be—of his own rare and elaborate species—"in his head". *Can* it have been as many as seven? Whatever the phrase precisely means, they must also have shared his heart, his life and his solar plexus. It looks as if *time*—the almanac's—has very little to do with the life of fiction, while it is in the womb, so to speak. Dates little matter.

And so (though this involves a steep descent from *The Turn of the Screw* and *The Aspern Papers*) with the tales that follow. Most of them have passed through changes—seldom rich, alas, but occasionally strange. Some of them are middle-aged. And, worse, may only too clearly look it. Most have been revised repeatedly; while some were born all but spick and span, only a springtime or so ago. One of them, cut down by half, actually came into being when Queen Victoria was still on the throne. Some of them, finally, in a slightly different shape, have been "on the air", and many have been serialized.

Very few, however, either in their character, their

settings, incidents, or themes, have had or have any positive actuality in conscious recollection or in view; though this cannot of course ransom them from being tarred with the same brush.

That so old a hand (even in the act of anathematizing it) should have immensely enjoyed the hard labour thus involved is nothing to the point perhaps; except that no man can take any deep or enduring pleasure in this world in a thing he has little "care" for. Here and there, and now and then, indeed, I should be hard put to it to declare which I care for most—the "actual" or the "imagined".

W.J.dlM.

June 1955

ODD SHOP

A silence, peculiar to itself, seemed to possess the little dark shop in the back street running up from the river—the silence, as it were, of intent listeners. It was suddenly shattered by the muffled ringing of a little verdigrised bell hanging up in the corner, and a chance visitor groping his way down its two wooden steps at once perceived it, became indeed curiously aware of it when the hospitable jangle had fallen into silence.

Nothing happened during the two or three minutes short of one o'clock that followed, leaving practically nothing behind them except the sense of their moments of peace and quiet and vague mystery. He then ventured an apologetic rap on the wooden counter. A few moments afterwards an old man quietly and carefully emitted himself through the glazed and curtained door of the shop parlour. He raised his chin and paused, having scrutinized, as far as his spectacles permitted, his visitor.

"Good afternoon, sir," he said. "What may I have the pleasure of doing for you?"

Odd Shop

"Good afternoon," returned his visitor, who realized he had taken a sudden fancy to the old gentleman. "I'm sorry to trouble you, but as a matter of fact I came to ask my way—to the railway station. I am a stranger here. You haven't, I see, lit up yet, and I am rather wishing I had brought a torch with me. I have been peering and peering through your little square windows but couldn't make out—not clearly—what is behind them. Are they cages? Extremely small, surely? For humming birds, I should imagine. . . . There is a thick mist rising."

Shopkeeper Yes, sir, we lie close to the river here; indeed this street brings you to its strand. I'm sorry you couldn't see in at the window, and glad that you didn't stumble on the two wooden steps. . . . You said "cages". In a sense, sir, you guessed rightly; cages they are. And yet, well, not for birds. There is very little trade just now; in fact you are my first customer—visitor, I should say —to-day. By good fortune I am not dependent on what I sell. By very good fortune, since what little business I used to do has been of late—well, sir, just washed out. As if the river itself had come flowing into the shop and swept me away. I have competitors—rich and powerful ones. And fashions change.

Customer The whole world has changed in these last few years including 'the sun'. The general aim, and scale. . . . Might I look at one of the little—er— cages?

Shopkeeper By all means, sir.

Odd Shop

Customer Thank you. What minute and exquisite workmanship! Charming. Is it of wood? Ivory? Metal? Tortoise-shell? Empty, anyhow.

Shopkeeper No, sir, not exactly empty. I choose colour and material according to the kind. Put it to your ear, sir, if I may be so bold, and merely press your finger—very lightly—on the minute knob at the corner. And—listen.

Customer Remarkable! A sound like someone rasping on a rough surface with a finger-nail. But shriller; more musical.

Shopkeeper There is a good deal of rasping on rough surfaces, nowadays. Fingers scratching their way out. But no, what you hear is only the call and possibly colloquy of a house cricket. Less frequent than it used to be, when the small country bakers' shops used to do their own bread-baking—and the Sunday pies and legs of mutton. A strange, simple, little sound; though not so simple as it seems. It is a nocturnal hymn, a love call. Poets, musicians, make love tunes, love songs. Most human beings talk their love—another kind of tune, sir. The cricket apparently rubs his thighs together, and the noise sounds out small, rough, shrill, even sonorous in the silence of midnight. I should explain, sir, that this is a Sound shop. I deal, I mean, solely in sounds; but chiefly in minute sounds. Those little heeded, little listened to. Here is another, if you will press the knob.

Customer Thank you. I can guess this one. A small child tapping very softly with her knuckle at her doll's-house door, I should think. (He mimics.) "Come in, come in, come in!"

Shopkeeper Not precisely, sir. That is the knocking of the death-watch beetle. Another love call, or summons to its mate. With its head, sir; though as it happens it knocks elsewhere at times—at the listener's heart. No, I am not suggesting that these trifles of mine are of any particular use. They are intended rather for what delight they may give—to the possessor. And this not merely for what they are in themselves, but for the states of mind which at different times they may evoke. An air on a fiddle may at one moment have less than little influence on us, and at another may be almost unendurably pathetic and moving.

Customer You said just now that the cricket's chirrup was a simple sound. This beats even that. But why "not so simple as it seems"? I think those were the words you used.

Shopkeeper I mean, as I have said, sir, that it is not so much what a sound is in itself, or even what causes it, that matters. But its effects. What it does to the listener. The tapping of the beetle first reminded you of a solitary child in a nursery, knocking and knocking to be let in to its own imagination, to its own profound fancy of its own small world of the doll's house. When you knew it for what it actually was, I warrant you saw quite a different picture, sir. Some definite tragic memory, perhaps—a pure superstition, of course. Each minute effect on the ear has evoked, one might

14

almost say, a minute panorama—or an extensive one, for that matter. A complete complicated little network of memories, perhaps. Isn't that so? That was what I had in mind. . . . I have a little box here containing three successive chords of music—powerful and possibly pregnant ones, from an opera by Wagner. But I wager it won't awaken more effective or deeper memories than the beetle. It isn't merely size that counts. Not just bare-faced noisy magnitude. . . . Gracious me, sir, this mist will soon be fog! Have you far to go? Now, sir, try this one. Two compartments, you will notice. First the little yellow knob. (The customer takes the box and puts it to his ear. A stare of astonishment transfigures his face.) Ah ha! I thought that might startle us a little. No mistaking that one, sir?

Customer My poor skull is fairly ringing. It sounds as if all the witches in hell were screaming to an obbligato from the old Father of Lies himself. Belial, Beelzebub and all the rest of them.

Shopkeeper No, sir, purely terrestrial. Merely a gale on the coast of Wales, near the great cathedral of St. David's, sir. Wind, wave, foam, sea-birds, shingle. A complex, but still a simple sound. We have very faint and slight notions, sir, of the lower regions—in spite of John Milton's help. I agree that a little closer listening might detect in the box the crash of some poor wretched bark and its inmates flung into the darkness of eternity on the starless rocks of night. But. . . . Now sir, the other button, the green one.

Customer Lovely! Like molten precious stones. As if you could turn dew into music. Water, of course; falling into—well, I wouldn't like to guess the depth of the well. An astonishing sense of solitude too. As of some incredibly old garden. The mists of daybreak and the silence of morning before the song of the bird. Fascinating.

Shopkeeper Well, well, sir. You would hardly believe it, but I spent over a week, a very happy one too, of twelve-hour working-days, on that one specimen. And yet, one wouldn't have to look very far to find the Well you mention. It is not at the world's end. The sound itself is merely that of milk dripping drop by drop from a teaspoon into a tea-cup. Completely domesticated!—but how the mind roves! That's what I mean by simple, sir. Now, if you please, this. This needs particularly close attention.

Customer I hear nothing. Yes, yes I do. A remote rustling. As of a ghost, I should imagine—approaching some unfortunate listener—not a child, I hope—down a long corridor. "Like one who on a lonely road." . . .

Shopkeeper No, sir, at least a league too far again. That is nothing less commonplace or more natural than the whisper an evening primrose makes when its petals—first gradually, then, as if its very being had so decided,—unfurl in the cool of the evening, exposing their riches to the prowling moths. That one yonder needs perhaps a closer attention; if, I mean, we leave it as Nature ordained. It enshrines the first stirrings of hoar-frost, its crystals gathering on a blade of grass. And these are the tiny brandishings of the antennae of a group of ants clustered in converse around their queen. . . . But I am detaining you. Still, here, sir—I feel sure it will interest you—is what I should call—well, it is different from the rest. And it costs me many a laborious day. I won't mention names, sir, since it is a matter of extreme privacy. It cost a friend of mine his son. My friend refused what he wanted of him, and his son left him. Left him. The little black knob, if you please.

Customer Yes, yes, I hear it. Very curious. Words. Stubborn, yet wavering. Tragic.

(He repeats what he hears in a low, cold, small, unfaltering voice.) *No, no, it can't be done. It can't be done. No, no, not even for him. It can't be done. Not even for him. It can't, it can't be done.*

Shopkeeper I would not part from that one for love or money. Not that a sale is likely. As I say, I have few visitors even, quite apart from customers, nowadays.

Customer Who was talking in that last one? Some old Jezebel, I should think. Some Fairy Devil-Mother.

Shopkeeper No, sir. It is many years old. It was the voice of conscience. And yet I am still a little uncertain that it wasn't the voice of what they call the ego, sir. The self far within us. I cannot say. As you see, there are many others. Quite common things, every one: even if not very familiar. But I mustn't be keeping you. Turn to the right as you leave this shop, take the first turning on the left, the third to the right, and you will find the station in a cul-de-sac down the third turning yet again to your right. No, sir, I am not allowed to sell at this hour. The shutters should have been up an hour ago. Against the law, sir. I do little more now than open and shut by habit. But it would be a pleasure to me if you would kindly accept this, merely as a little remembrance of this evening. This one is the voice of advancing age, sir; hardly articulate. Yes, there is the knob.

Customer No—nothing. Yes, I detect a voice, but—it's too far away: only a murmur; no distinguish-able syllables.

Shopkeeper I fancied that might be the case. I myself am accustomed to it. And yet—well it goes like this.

(He speaks in faint, yet clear and sorrowful tones.) *Snow, dust, motes of light, falling time, time ever falling. Remember, yes, remember. Oh, yes, remember. Yes, remember.*

Customer (A little bitterly.) That's all very well! But I should have supposed rather than "remember", look ahead. Do you ever listen—in?

Shopkeeper Bless you, sir, I am years behind the times: behind my times, too. But yet I might say that I am always listening in. But not yet, please God, to what they call "voices". Indeed, I have hardly a moment now to spare from a last little

job which I fear I shall never finish, a night job
too. I am endeavouring, quite between ourselves,
if I may venture, to distinguish and to capture the
music of the spheres. Very old-fashioned. The
morning stars. But alas, with no success. Not yet.
. . . Thank you, sir. I haven't tied the string
tightly, and perhaps it would be advisable to carry
the little parcel, not to put it into the pocket.
Good night, sir, and many thanks.

He watches his visitor mount the narrow street and
vanish into the thickening fog. No one, not even
a cat, is otherwise in sight. The no one, indeed,
might almost have been nothing. Merely an old man's
memory—after the muffled jangling of the shop-bell
had ceased.

MUSIC

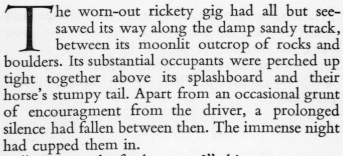

The worn-out rickety gig had all but see-sawed its way along the damp sandy track, between its moonlit outcrop of rocks and boulders. Its substantial occupants were perched up tight together above its splashboard and their horse's stumpy tail. Apart from an occasional grunt of encouragment from the driver, a prolonged silence had fallen between then. The immense night had cupped them in.

"How much further now?" his passenger at length inquired.

"Better part of a mile, maybe."

"The old mare goes well."

"Ay."

"It's fortunatate you brought the gig. Few of my patients telephone me until there is urgent need; and wet sand over rocks makes risky going for a car. You can snap an axle that way....Telephones appear not to be very fashionable hereabouts?"

"The master doesn't care for cars. Or telephones neether. He has no need for them. As for the going, it's a sight better here than it may be nearer home."

There was no surliness in the voice, only a kind of tired patience.

"Well," said the other, glancing seawards, "I am not familiar with this coast-track. You'd suppose no mortal creature had ever visited it before. Nor had I a notion that the dunes were so steep and lofty here. It's like some outlandish desert. Strange." It seemed he might have been talking to himself.

"Ay," came the answer. "So it is to most. We lie out of the way, like. And well worth while—if there's not too much of it."

"Have *you* been here long?"

"With where I am? About fifteen years. And this will be the last of them." The tone had become muffled, as though the speaker were uncertain to add, Thanks be! or precisely its opposite.

"You are leaving Dr. Brandt, then? It *was* 'Doctor', you said?"

No sound followed the question for a while except the swish of the descending sea-wet sand from the rims and spokes of the high wheels, and the hiss of the incoming tide. A few stars were shining between the thin flat layers of cloud in the sky.

"He's leaving *me*, is Dr. Brandt," came the answer at last. "There's no hope for him."

"You didn't tell me that when you rang the house-bell some little time ago. Was there 'hope' do you suppose *then*? This afternoon?"

The driver drew his head a little further down into his coat collar. "I wasn't bid come then . . . Dr.

Brandt *asked* for you. That's not his way, and that's why I came. But to my thinking he doesn't really want you. Unless, maybe, to say his last. He's used to being ill. He knows. He's old—and tired. I've nothing to say against him; far from it. He's a bit queer, though; just now. It's this music-stuff that's on his mind. He thinks of nothing else; he broods on it. And so, I suppose, he can't die easy."

His passenger ignored a good deal in these remarks that might have tempted anyone less professionally reticent.

"I see. It's music then that is Dr. Brandt's hobby? A composer, I suppose?"

"Yes; if that's what you call them. A composer. Music. There are rows and rows of these books of his in the house. Funny-looking stuff. Scribbled along lines, and most of it, without a word of writing from cover to cover. Though there *may* be words too now and then. Songs, I suppose. In the old days he'd sit for an hour or more together, or longer; without a finger stirring—until his pen was dry."

"What does he do now, then?" inquired his passenger, as if he were a little apprehensive of intruding too much, although he had had time to think his question over before asking it.

"He's always listening."

" 'Listening'? What does he listen to?"

"To everything. . . . Because of this music."

"But you haven't said what music," replied the doctor, without revealing the irritability he might be feeling, his eyes peering out to the horizon-line over the waste watery hummocks of the sea. "I don't follow you."

"Well, listen then. . . . *Whoa*!"

The creaking wheels slowly ceased to revolve, and, with their human burden, came to a standstill. The clock-like hoof-beats ceased. And a vast mellay, as though of shouts, cries, multitudes, at once filled to overflowing the spaces around them, like the bubbling and simmering of a gigantic pot of broth. So multitudinous and continual was the clamour of the leaden-grey mass of water, stretching out here to the rim of the globe, it would seem that earthly night could never be silent. And this was accompanied by immense mutterings and echoings out of the starry vacancies above it. The mare, with a cough and a shudder, suddenly shook her whole ramshackle body so violently that every metal buckle of her worn-out harness rang and rattled again.

"Oh, that," said the doctor, as if in sudden enlightenment. "The roar, the rocks, the billowing breakers. You call *that* 'music', then? Surely, that could not delude or distress anyone accustomed to it—well or ill! The whistling and siffling of wind and sand over the dunes, the tide washing and ruckling in the shingle. Is *that* Dr. Brandt's trouble?"

The driver shrugged his rounded shoulders.

" 'Twasn't me that made any mention of 'trouble'," he replied flatly, "that's your word." And once again they fell silent—and listened in a brief lull in the noise of wind and water to the barking of a dog from some inland farmyard, and the faint blast of a ship's siren far out to sea.

"*That*", he went on ironically, "was the old retriever bitch at Farmer Hallows's, that was. And the ship is making for Kellsay Harbour."

"You have good ears."

"Ay, and need them."

"You listen *too*, then—to this 'music', as you call it?"

"You'd be stone-deaf not to *hear* it. And there are many as are. I *listen* only because I'm told to. What you seem to be talking of is not the 'music' neether. Not what Dr. Brandt finds in it, anyway. He says that even this criss-cross hullabaloo that's all around us has a meaning to it, if one could give it a name. What he's after is different. And there I'm useless. Nor wishing to be anything else. . . . Why, you can listen to your own ears, in a manner of speaking. But you'd better not give heed to fancies —to what as like as not, isn't there. There are some who say they hear 'voices'. You wouldn't, p'raps," he added slyly, "wish me to share them I suppose. . . . Come up, lass."

The sea-foam swept as though furtively a little nearer to the track, and the gig lurched slowly forward on its melancholy journey. The doctor drew up the collar of his great-coat.

"Much further now? . . . It's coldish. What does your Master *say* about this music? He is gravely ill, I understand."

" 'Ill'," his companion echoed dryly. "I keep a-telling you, he's all but past it. Not, mind you, that I wouldn't do the best I can for him. But you have to make a stand somewhere. For his own sake. He says it's in the air. But then he could tell you the name of any bird—land-bird or sea-bird—you might have heard warbling, or screeching, why, half a mile off. He can hear a fly crawl over the wall. He can watch even a trace of a lie in your mouth before a syllable comes out of it, as easy as a cat catches mice. Things said to him and meant only for kindness, I mean. The truth is, under the sheets, sometimes, he dreads—he is afeared—of this music. You'd almost think he was hiding his eyes to escape from it. That's the truth. Sometimes. Not always. Mostly, it's meat and drink to him—and no living soul to share it."

"In the air, you say?" repeated the doctor. "He maintains that this music is in the air, does he? Nothing connected with fancies about wireless, I suppose?"

"'Wireless'!" muttered the driver derisively, and spat sideways out of the gig. "What would he be doing with that stuff. God help us, do you mean what they call this jazz? Try a race-horse with musty offal. No, not that. It's his *own* music; wherever that comes from. Whether it's what they call *audible* or not. Travellers say, he once told me, there's something of the sort to be heard even in the middle of these great empty deserts they tell of. Out in the East, there. Harps, drums, dulcimers and the like. Others say it's caused by the heat and the shifting of the sands. After a hell-hot day or when the wind's in

the driest quarter. You'll never fail of finding a wise-
acre these days who couldn't tell you whether your
eyes are shut or not when you're asleep!" He wiped
his mouth with the back of his hand; and smiled. "I
expect they learn it in these books! *He* listens; ay,
his lips moving perhaps, and a smile on his old face
like a child asking for a slice of bread and sugar. Or
he used to. It's in all such lonely god-forsaken parts
as these, he says. Ay, and those out of the ship-
tracks. And it's not of this earth at all. That's what
he says. And that, off and on, he has been waiting
for it—listening—all his life. And I shouldn't wonder if it has got into those music books of his, either.
All lines and squiggles—like this Persian and Chinese.
The truth is, the poor gentleman's gone a bit crazy
in his wits; that's the truth. Bats in the belfry—*and*
bells. But as calm and pleasant about it all as a baby
in its cradle. And a gentleman if ever there was one.
And sweeter in temper, and less hasty than he used
to be. . . ."

He broke off suddenly. They had turned a little
inland, round one of the dunes, then out again
towards the sea and the rocks.

"There's the house!" he bawled in the tumult that
followed, pointing with his whip. "Over there,
where the moon is shining."

"Gad! Is it!" muttered his companion. "You're
right." He continued for a while to stare at the glass-
panes of its windows, shot with the blaze of the
moon. . . . "A solitary place, and no mistake. Curious. With that silvery shining glitter on the slates it is

hardly distinguishable from the sand themselves. Are there other servants? A nurse? Many relatives?"

"Servants?—no. Ten or a dozen rooms, I suppose, all told. Some of them all but empty. And then there's the kitchen and those parts. . . . There's a brother. He never comes this way now, though. As I've said, except for the woman who does for the old gentleman from the village, all he has is me. And you may well say, solitary. When extra high water swims up all around us here—we are marooned, as they say. He *began* this music-talk months—ay, years ago. It gets on your nerves in time. You wouldn't, else, I guess, catch your*self*, listening too. And as often as not in the dark."

His companion—his head turning slowly sidelong —scrutinized his features ruminatingly. "Well, I'm glad *you're* not another patient. You must have been a great and constant help to Dr. Brandt. This trouble which we now call 'nerves' is the folly of the age. It's the froth of the life we lead; and none too whole-some at that. . . . Does Dr. Brandt ever describe these illusions? To others? We are most of us subject to something of the sort. Every city in the world has its own voice you might say. Every wilderness and churchyard too; every human memory is haunted by *some* voice. Or by silence."

The driver treated his passenger to a prolonged stare.

"You ask me, 'Does he say what it's *like*'? Well, you'd suppose at times he heard the angels singing. And at other times, *not* the angels. By God, no.

Music

Brassy trumpets, horns, cymbals, kettle-drums, and the like. With all those bookfuls of his own music, it's nothing but his own imaginings and fancies, I tell him. To keep him quiet. . . . Crazy, poor gentleman, or not, he won't be forgotten. I'll lay you that. Sometimes, to humour him, I say it's all out of the past. Hollows in the air. Relics, as you might call them. Why not? There's a full-sized church under the sands over yonder. When my grandfather was a boy he used to listen to its bells. Now, when there's a winter sea riding in, it's like an army of cavalry, cannon and shouting. Of a soft summer night, too, he'll lie there, quietly smiling to himself. Mermaids, p'raps! Like as if he was a child again and his nannie telling him stories and combing his hair. For people cooped up in towns and suchlike, such things are merely book-stuff nowadays; and these lying cheap-jacknewspapers."

The old mare's hoofs steadily and hollowly thudded on with an occasional spark struck by a shoe from a half-hidden flint. He brooded a while.

"Mind you," he went on, "you get your ears sharpened—listening. There are three dogs hereabouts, all within whistle, though you wouldn't think it. And I could tell you which of them's howling down the moon, with a horse-cloth tied over my head. And the cocks bawling at midnight, near and far: you can hear 'em fading out half across the county. You get—well, as you might say, *open* to it, by trying. And Dr. Brandt, he's *wide*-open to it. That's the only difference; or near it. And then you

begin fancying. . . . *Whoa*, Nancy, girl! She shies
and stumbles at that lump of rock every time we
passes it. P'raps she *sees* things. And here we are. I'll
tie her up for the time being. You won't have to be
long, I reckon. Perhaps a look'll be enough. I'll go
in first and turn up the lamp, though there's moon
enough for a funeral."

He reappeared in the solid faded doorway, and the
doctor followed him down and across a wide corridor, with pictures on its walls, into a room at the
back of the house. He paused at a high window.

"My word!" he all but muttered. "What a view!
And what a tide coming in! . . . No mistaking *that*
music! And if you add, 'Bats in the belfry'. . . .
Well?"

He had turned towards his companion, only to
find himself alone, and that he had been conversing,
with no one to answer. The glass in the uncurtained
lofty window-sashes with their heavy shutters, can
only have slightly diminished the tumultuous rever-
berations of the sea. The whole house seemed to be
gently trembling in the vibrations of air and water.
Far to the south, along the rugged coast, a light reiteratedly blinked at this stranger. Footsteps at length
sounded again, and Dr. Brandt's factotum re-entered
the room.

"He seems to be asleep. Fast. I whispered him
close up. He's dreaming—or looks like it. His bald
old face—handsome in a way—was as calm as a
tombstone. . . . I'm desperate sorry he's going.
Will you wait here, or shall I wake him? Better not

until it's needed. There's a barrel of beer in the kitchen, and food in the larder. Ay, he said before you came that I was to make you comfortable and at home, and all that. 'At home'!"

"No beer, thank you. Has your master a fire? It's a comfortless night in spite of the moon. Because, perhaps. . . . Just now, while you were gone—*ssh!* Listen!"

He had stayed his talk, interrupted as it seemed by a perceptible change in the resounding churning of noise, rumour and echo beyond the walls of the house. There had accompanied it, too, what seemed like a gabble, or, rather a remote yet vaguely harmonical babble of voices, either high up or in the interstices of the hiss and clutter of the sea.

"Is *that* it?" he inquired sharply. "Is that anything like what he means? Yet surely that too is only the in-and-out, the surge and swish of the sandy water in the hollows of the rocks; and the wind's far-away trumpetings. Strange, though!"

The morose answer to his question seemed needlessly resonant and argumentative in the silent house itself—

"*You* can hear what you like. *I* say, that's all deceiving. What's strange in a following wind and a spring tide coming in? Fast, too. It—it's a real bumper," he added ironically. "you'll have plenty of time for whatever needs doing. It will be all around us before the clock strikes; and it isn't *we* who will be able to hie off then."

"Well, you live here; you are familiar with all

this, and you should know. But there certainly was a sound then, the like of which I cannot recall having heard, either from wind *or* water. Not that I haven't lived by the sea. Dr. Brandt hasn't any instrumental devices that may not be known to you, I suppose? Things I mean for his own amusement, and for his own ear only?"

"Haven't I told you, no, again and again! Apart from his old pyanniforty over there, and that crammed cupboard in the corner, there's nothing else I've ever seen. And he hasn't opened eether of them for months past. I tell you, I'm sick and tired of the whole thing and shall be glad when—when I'm gone. All I'm asking now is a quiet end for the old gentleman, or I wouldn't have come for you. I shall be at an empty end myself, let alone a loose one, when he's gone. I tell you I'm *attached* to him, and can't bear the thought of his weakening and waning. A quiet end, that's what'd be his greatest earthly blessing."

"Certainly," said his visitor. "But you couldn't but have come, if you were told to. As for a quiet end, that's neither here nor there. You can depend on me to do my best for Dr. Brandt."

"Ay. So say all the others. What *I* am saying is, if we have to go, why not go easy? Would you keep even a cat alive, its eyes green with a poisoned liver?"

The doctor remained silent, his eyes fixed on the distant and revolving lantern of the lighthouse, repeatedly obscured by the tossing surf.

"But surely," he began persuasively at last, "aren't we beating about the bush? All that you say, I agree, is kindly meant. Concerning Dr. Brandt's sick fancies of this music; though scarcely this talk of 'others'. It's not for us to criticize what we cannot understand. And that is immeasurable! A great, rare and unusual mind has its own pathways to follow. If they are not ours, what wonder? And what *then*? . . . How often does this music, which even we ourselves may think at times we hear, as if between waking and sleeping —how often does it occur, or seem to occur? At set times? At certain states of the weather, of the tides perhaps? Why is it sometimes pleasing, and at others—what you said—alarming? Terrifying? Has anyone else heard it! What do you yourself think its cause to be?"

"Answer for question, that's a mouthful, and no mistake! And you can leave what *I* think of the master to me. We trust one another. I won't even go for to allow it *is* music—more, at least, than all that tumbling and roaring there beyond the window, and which these old chimneys perhaps could part explain. It comes one night; and then not again. Once in June—a summer's afternoon, and that whole hedge there of honeysuckle in bloom, and he sitting proud as a child—it seemed there was a-harping near all around us in the warm sweet air; and that's what he said. And what its cause?—no more than the insects and the sea-ripplings and the birds, and the breeze in the hot stones of the wall. I've talked and I've argyfied, and I've *not* talked. I've had my say; and now this is the end. And then *you* come along", he all but jeered, "and chatter about the weather and states of the tide. As if I couldn't draw a map of the place, ocean and all, and rocks for the sea-maids? In my sleep! I ask you! How could anybody else have heard if there's none to listen? Or none with, as you might say, the innocence. To believe even their *own* ears, maybe.

"By God!"—it seemed he had almost shouted, though he had scarcely raised his voice, "that's just where you are mistaken. That's just where you are jumping though you haven't anything to jump from. Louder! different! louder! You may think, if you want to, that it's *my* tiles that are loose. Who cares? What he says, what the old man, what my old master in there, *says*, is that there will come a moment, and pretty soon maybe, when nothing human could *stay* to listen: neither choice nor power. There'll come a crack, a burst of it, a sound like some almighty threat of thunder; only *music*, mind you, that may snap your backbone and stun you for good and all. That's what he says. And then p'raps, he looks at me, sad and smiling for all the world as if he had gone back to his mother's apron-strings again. And next moment he's trembling and half-scared like a lost dog, and longing only for sleep. And he has not had any real sweetening bout of that that I could mention for three days or more. He——"

He had been interrupted.

"What's that over there? By the door there?" had interjected the doctor.

a   33

"That," was the contemptuous reply, "that's a cat, that is." He stooped and softly snapped his fingers towards the shadowy creature in the dusk. "This here", he cajoled, "is the Doctor, Fanny. Come to see Master, he has. Shake hands. . . . *She's* a listener, too. Look at her! Ah, she's gone."

In the pause that followed there sounded out of the back parts of the house a low desolate caterwauling, and then a faint ethereal echo, as of some child's home-made little harp, and then other stranger, more sonorous instruments, rising and falling, yet as though unintentionally, with the myriad sighings and sifflings of the sea.

"Well, there's no mistaking that," said the doctor. "And it is meeting together too. And I take back what I said. There are those who talk of elementals. And they might easily be alarming—alone here. Or, as some might say, it is the house that is haunted. It is a sea house. It is the place itself and its past. It entices these visitations, and so affects our human sensibilities." He seemed to have begun talking to himself. "We have only a short stay in this world. We can but listen, and . . ."

"And *I* say, I tell you, it's only imagining. My poor old master is dying in there. He's music-mad. What's more, tide in, there'll be an end to it. And with the ebb, which should be about a quarter to four, he'll be gone. Shall you still be waiting? Or shall I take you in to him?"

The doctor hesitated, "If you are sure he's quiet and sleeping, I will wait. Besides, to judge from the look of the sea, the tide by now must be well over the track. Best not to disturb him. Look in again, in a few minutes' time."

He turned towards the man with a faint smile, almost as if they were old friends.

"This seems to be a strange and very solitary house. Do you ever *see* anything?"

"Old as the Ark; and about as seaworthy! 'See' things? That's easy if you shut your eyes. And what's the difference with listening? It's neether common sense nor natural. And who listens, nowadays? These roaring crazy towns. Who ever *stops* talking in 'em. Why, there's not enough talk in this house in a month to last a rookery for half an afternoon. I'm dog-sick of it. What I said to myself, coming along in the gig, was: You keep your mouth shut, my son! You keep your teeth locked over your tongue. Let the medicine-man find out for himself. And there you go again, asking questions! And even now that you've had the answers, be damned if you haven't followed along the same road again. . . . Not that I'm minding!

"Put fancies into people's heads, I say, and they breed—or rot. Music! Give me a brass band or a hurdy-gurdy and I'm with you. But all this church palaver. All this flocking up of the quiet of the air, this talk of voices—the whole world over, they say. . . . I'm with the old man, every inch, mind you. I've done for him with these two hands day and night for fifteen years. And he's no lightweight now —to get him back into bed at times. I've borne with him, and no nurse could have done more. Nor his own mother neether. And never a word, except to you. But it will be a release for him, and I can take care of myself. As for this 'music'—strike me blind, deaf and dumb, before I'll say yes to that!"

For the few moments that followed, it seemed as though they had been listening to one another *not* talking. And the doctor began softly:

"I'm not denying a word you say. Why get beside ourselves? Nothing is lost by being civil—even to what is round us and may never answer back. I know. I realize it must have been a trying time for you. A thread running and knotting itself through your life. And you can depend on me to do my best. On the other hand, as I see myself, *now*. Nothing could be served by pretending that Dr. Brandt is merely a victim of what we call fancy. . . . Why, our own ears . . ."

There had followed the sound of a slow protracted gush, a seventh wave, of the inning tide; and yet again the hoot of a steamer's siren. And then, from out of the moonlit emptiness and huge vacancy of the night, steadily gathering, as if the very stars in their courses had stayed to listen, there followed a music—a music drawing nearer until the whole canopy of the heavens enveloping the world seemed to be welling with a vast strangely beautiful and terrifying strain of harmony. It died away like a falling rumour of itself into the wail of a rising wind and the incessant din of the breakers. . . . A kind of pallor appeared to have fallen on the two human faces, although the moon must have been on the other side of the house. . . .

"Someone is coming?"

"Ay, he's coming himself."

There followed, and seemingly from far away, yet distinct, a voice inquiring, "Is that you, Raven? Is that you? You are back? Are you alone? I'm here; I'm coming. It doesn't matter now. It is only to thank you and say that I shall not want you any more. I have heard . . . nothing wrong now. You must get back to sleep, Raven. . . ."

THE STRANGER
A DIALOGUE.

The midday sunshine is flooding through the french windows of the little parlour as it is called—and almost as if, furtively, revealing colour by colour the pattern of the carpet on the floor. The only occupant of the room is sitting at the piano—her back to the window—a girl in her earlier teens. She is pale, dark-haired, grey-eyed, and at this moment, pensive. Her thoughts are far away as she continues slowly ruining the opening bars of "When other lips and other hearts Their tales of love shall tell". However clumsy she may be at the moment, she is engrossed; but after yet another heartrending discord her hands fall to her lap and she sits motionless for the few moments before her mother enters the room. She is breathless but speaks in a low "inward" voice rapidly and impulsively.

Mother Where *have* you been, Sheelagh? When did you come in? You are nearly three-quarters of an hour late. I have been wandering about everywhere—to meet you. And since that poor child—. . . . And those wretched motor cars. You are so heedless, so headstrong,—in everything,—

The Stranger

Sheelagh I'm sorry, Mother. But I hadn't any more pennies to pay the tram fare.

Mother But surely, child, I can't have forgotten giving—.

Sheelagh Yes, but I mean *back*, Mother.

Mother Back from where?

Sheelagh I don't see why you should be so cross about it. I just went . . . I was carried on too far.

Mother Too far? What can you mean? In the tram? What were you doing? Learning a lesson? How can you have been so foolish—so absent-minded?

Sheelagh I'm sorry, Mother. We got right up past Beulah Road before I realized. (Scornfully.) "Learning a lesson", indeed! Of course not. I shouldn't have mentioned it if I thought you'd make such a fuss about it—I was talking to someone.

Mother "Talking to someone"? Who? A friend? But didn't *she* tell you that you had gone beyond the stopping place? . . . What were you talking about?

Sheelagh It wasn't a "she", Mother. It was a man.

Mother A man! Who? What kind of man?

Sheelagh A stranger, Mother. *Kind* of man?—why, our kind of man, of course.

Mother Look, Sheelagh. Have I never told you that it is never advisable to talk to any stranger, and particularly. . . . It doesn't matter a bit—man or woman. What should anyone want to talk to a schoolgirl for?

Sheelagh I don't see why *not* to a schoolgirl. After

all, I'm not a child. Besides, I didn't talk to him; he talked to me.

Mother I didn't say you were a child. I thought you had better sense. "Talked to *me*": you *know* that's merely quibbling. What did he talk to you about? What was he like? Have you seen him before?

Sheelagh O, Mother! All those questions. I don't *think* I've ever seen him before. And yet—I don't know quite how to describe the feeling. How can one tell? For certain? I may have. He wanted to pay my fare back, but I wouldn't let him.

Mother Of course not. Did he get out, or . . .

Sheelagh When I did? Yes, I should think he walked about two lamp-posts with me. Then he went on the other way.

Mother I asked you what he talked to you about. You say he was a gentleman? How could he, in that case. . . . What was he like?

Sheelagh As if I didn't know a gentleman by this time! He was dark—very dark, except his eyes. He had blue eyes. And no one could possibly have been nicer, more polite, I mean. And I'm sure you'd agree, Mother, he was *very* good-looking.

Mother Very good-looking! Good heavens, child! What have good looks to do with it?

Sheelagh But I didn't say they *had*, Mother. But it wasn't so much his face as his voice. I remember Daddie once saying that you can tell a person's character better by that than by anything else. Whether, I mean, one's telling the truth or not. I don't *think* he was quite English.

The Stranger

Mother Really, Sheelagh! You are being purposely provoking, just keeping everything back. Why didn't you say at once he was a foreigner. If only I had gone that way to meet you! It never even occurred to me, though I knew you had left the School, because I telephoned. And what might *not* have become of you? You might have had a bad accident, been killed. For all I knew. . . . Oh, Sheelagh!

Sheelagh But even if I had, I don't see why it must have been my *fault*. Besides, *then*, you might not have heard *yet*. And he wasn't a foreigner. All I meant was that he didn't speak—well, just like most people. It was a little like Miss O'Reilly's brother, the gym mistress. (*There is a pause, and Sheelagh begins faintly strumming her tune again.*)

Mother (In a low, tense voice.) Miss O'Reilly? She's Irish, isn't she? Do you mean. . . ? (Angrily.) Will you please stop strumming that silly sentimental song and turn your face to me. I don't want to be hasty, and I'm not hurt in any way. But you keep on evading my questions. What did this stranger talk to you *about*?

Sheelagh I hope you don't mean that, *because* my back was turned, I was telling lies. I wouldn't tell lies with my back turned, anyhow. And you didn't say it was a silly song when we heard it the other day—. I saw you listening. "*Talk* to me?" The stranger in the tram? I'm sure, for one thing, he wouldn't have at all—if he had known this would happen. How silly it all is! A book slipped off my lap, my French book, and he picked it up and smiled at me. He came in immediately after me. He said it was a lovely day. And so it was, Mother; look at the sun! I saw the first May-tree in bloom this morning: and you could hear the birds, the thrushes, even in the tram. I agree, Mother, he did stare rather. But not a bit in a horrid way. And then I thought he wasn't going to say anything more. And, well, I was sorry. But at last he turned back from looking out at the driver and asked me what School I came from.

Mother Oh! Sheelagh, how can you have been so foolish—so, so unwise!

Sheelagh You won't let me go on. Of course, I told him the School. Why, the letters are on my hat. And then he asked me if I was going home, and how old I was, and when my birthday was. Perhaps he'll send me a lovely present. Wouldn't that be fun? *You'd* choose a doll for your little girl! Oh, do be a sport, Muzzie dear.

Mother (In rapid anxious tones.) Listen, darling. Please don't joke and be silly. If you had had my ex—if you knew, I mean, what I know of this world, you'd realize that I had cause for being uneasy, anxious. It's *because* you are not a child, and so trustful and impulsive, and just follow your heart and not your head. And I don't mean that you shouldn't, but. . . . What did he say then?

Sheelagh He looked at me, and smiled. And then he asked me where I lived.

Mother And you *told* him?

Sheelagh Well, I did wonder a little at that. Then I remembered that after all he only had to follow me to find out. Besides, as I keep on saying, I knew he was just—just being kind. And after that, well, we talked—almost as if we were old friends. He asked me what I should like to do when I left School, and whether I should be able to. He said, "You look very happy. Are you?" That *was* rather queer, wasn't it? Of course, I'm happy—generally.

Mother Follow you! Kind! Happy! I can't think what girls you can have been mixing with—putting things into your head like that. And now you are turning your back again. I'm dreadfully tired, I must sit down and rest a minute.

Sheelagh I was only looking in the glass, Mother. Mummie, *dear*! And you do that yourself, don't you? sometimes? I've watched you. You purse your lips like this, and turn your head first to one side and then to the other. And *I* think you look adorable. It's just then, if I was a man, I'd fall in love with you! And I suppose you'll think it's only horrid conceit or something if—well, *do* dark hair and blue-grey eyes—like, like mine—often go together? Miss O'Reilly has greenish eyes. *Your* eyes, Mother, are brown—like pansies. And I adore them; and you know that I wouldn't for the world let the tiniest cloud. . . . There, don't let's say anything more. Please.

Mother I'm asking you to be serious, Sheelagh. I don't *like* this man. He *can't* have been a gentle-

43

man. Did you tell him your name? Surely you
must have known. . . . And you confided in him
—a perfect stranger—that you were happy? And
what have eyes and hair to do with that?

Sheelagh Yes, I did. You wouldn't wish me to have
told him a fib about that surely. I wanted to ask
him *his* name. That would have been only fair.
But I didn't like to.

Mother Then he *did* ask you yours? What did you
say?

Sheelagh You just go on *telling* me what he said to
me! And he didn't ask me my name, either. He
guessed it—or saw it on my book. That was the
only other curious little thing. Because I don't
think—*now* I mean—that at first he wanted to
know anything about *me*! But about another girl!

Mother (Momentarily relieved.) Oh! Another girl.
Who?

Sheelagh Quite at the beginning, he asked me if I
had a school-fellow named Willing. He said he
once had an old friend who lived about here who
had a daughter, that this was his friend's name,
and he thought that perhaps. . . .

Mother *Willing!* You're absolutely sure that he said
Willing?

Sheelagh Why, of course! And I said what a very
curious thing it was that he should have asked me
that.

Mother Why—"curious"?

Sheelagh He smiled at me. And I said it was because
that name was once . . .

The Stranger

Mother (Prompting her.) "That name was once"
. . . ?

Sheelagh Oh, Mother, how can you be so slow? That
it was once *your* name. And I do think, considering how kind and how nice he was, and interested
—almost as if I was grown-up, I mean: I don't see
why you should judge him—or me—like that. I
wouldn't have dreamed of talking to him—because of what you once said—if he had been horrid or nosy or silly—that kind of thing. But he
wasn't. I *liked* him. I hoped then I might see him
again. But, now, how can I, after what you have
said? Why, I wouldn't be as suspicious and stand-
offish as that even to the Conductor. But there!
I suppose I mustn't, in future, say "Good morning" even to him.

Mother Sheelagh, I want you to be—I can't quite
say what I mean—but I want you always to realize
that I never tell you what to do or what not to
do unless I think—*know* it's for the best. There are
—dangers; even when everything . . . ourselves as
well as others. And although a supreme, a priceless blessing may . . . You see, life leads us on and on,
but there is always the *past*. You can never, never,
root out that. Never know when it may not rise
up again out of—out of its ashes. I am sure now,
from what you have told me, that, that—this
stranger hadn't any—any designs; nothing like
that. Still, I want you to promise that, for a few
days at any rate, you'll come home another way.
It will only mean your being a little later than

usual, and the walk will do you good. (*Gropingly* —*as if against her will.*) You say you liked him? Why? His voice? How did he look? (*Anxiously.*) Did he, did he say that he might be coming to see you? No, of course not.

Sheelagh Coming to see me? Mother, how silly! We just talked of anything and everything else that came into our heads after that. At least I did.

Mother After what?

Sheelagh After I had told him how odd it was he should have an old friend living about here called Willing—I mean, that it was your name.

Mother And what did he say then?

Sheelagh Nothing. Not at first. He looked at me as though he were waiting for me to go on. Then he turned away and then smiled at me again, as if *we* were old friends. And that is true, Mother, isn't it? I mean, *some* people—strangers—you seem to know almost at once, don't you? But I don't think it means past lives, do you? That was what I *felt*. And Daddy I'm sure . . .

Mother Daddy? What has Daddy to do with this? I can't imagine what he would say if he knew of it. You must promise me, Sheelagh—on no account —to tell him even a syllable of what you have confided in me. He'd never have a happy moment again if he felt that. . . . You promise?

Sheelagh If you ask. Of course, Mother.

Mother You say he, this stranger—looked *well*? Did he, did *he* seem happy, too?

The Stranger

Sheelagh Oh, Mother! He looked very well; and I believe if you and I had been together, and he'd begun to talk to *us*, we'd have laughed over it just like two cats. You would have loved it. And then it would have been *our* little secret! But I wouldn't say he had *always* been happy. When he asked about my childhood and, and the future, he looked almost as if he were homesick—well, you know what I mean—envious. I don't think, although there was a ring on his finger, that he was married. I don't *think* so.

(A little bell sounds.)

Mother That's luncheon—the second time.

Sheelagh You won't say anything to Miss Pearce, Mother, will you? I do wish you hadn't telephoned.

Mother No, I promise. He asked, you say, if *I* was happy? Didn't that strike you as curious?

Sheelagh I didn't say so. But he did. Not so very "curious". He was telling me about his having been abroad, and how gay and cheerful the people are. And you see, if, at the beginning I had told you what he said last—though you wouldn't give me a chance—you would have seen there couldn't have been anything silly or wrong in my talking to him. You know how fond I am of Daddy, but I do sometimes find it very hard—well, to say all that I mean—everything. I think he is always interested and yet . . . well, I'm sure he doesn't understand me, not quite as you do, you dear sweet thing. *He* listened—as if even a schoolgirl.

... Oh, Mother, do cheer up. I do wish you didn't look so pale and tired and—and troubled about this. There isn't the very least need to. And you know I'm sorry.

Mother Yes. But you mustn't, dearest, think like that about your father. He loves you—just as—as I do. But *he*—the stranger, what *did* he say "*last*"?

Sheelagh Why, he stayed silent a moment, and then he said, "Perhaps it would be as well to mention to your Mother that we've had this little talk. Especially as you have gone on too far with me. She may be anxious about you. Tell her that I have been away from England a long time and shall be leaving again soon. Say what a pleasure it has been to talk to you"—to *me*, Mother! "She will understand." Those were his very words. And I suppose *I* must have looked a little anxious, too. "Like Mother—like Daughter", he said, and smiled again. And we stood there under the Chestnut tree by Dr. Symmons's; and we shook hands and said "Good-bye". And I don't think he wanted to—not for always. And after a little, I looked back, and he was looking back; and we waved to one another. I am perfectly certain, Mother dear, you'd have liked him—immensely. But—well—I don't believe, somehow, that I shall ever see him again.

Mother No?

Sheelagh No, Mother.

Mother Sheelagh, my precious, precious one. Don't look at me like that! You know I would never,

The Stranger

never deny you a real friend. Never. It was—kind
of him to send me such a message. I am glad
now that you were outspoken, and your own
natural, impulsive self. It was only that at first I
was a little frightened, alarmed. . . . My precious
and precious! All these years! Why, you are crying, Silly; and—and so am I. God bless you. I must
run upstairs a moment. What *will* Jessie think of
us! I won't—I won't be long.

(She pauses as she opens the door, her slender
fingers on the painted china door-handle, her lips
apart as if she were about to speak again—an
ecstatic and passionate expression of tenderness,
sorrow, love, transfixing her beautiful face. But
she decides against doing so, and goes out.

NEIGHBOURS

Miss Guthrie's arduous day closed in complete lassitude. Body and mind alike relaxed utterly after its unusual intensity. It was Miss Pugh, indeed, who had hitherto originated: she herself had merely by incessant exertion deprived her rival of glory by instant imitative counter-stroke. To-day, however, had been spent in feverish hope that at last her own somewhat prosaic industry had stolen a march upon the curious placid genius she could not deny to her neighbour.

Well before it was usual or quite genteel to be abroad she had visited a distant florist, and carried off, roots and all, absolutely the newest of novelties in standard roses. The whole morning had then been spent in precise and secret preparations. And, at last, in late afternoon, when Miss Pugh, she felt assured, would be resting and out of sight of the two gardens, she had tugged on her old leather gardening gloves, dug the hole, trodden down the loam over the roots, and set the meagre glorious thing firmly upright in its place. Thence in the fullness of time it should advance to a triumph unsuspected until it was inevitable.

Neighbours

And now, worn-out, in petticoat and slippers, her "shocker" open and unheeded beneath her reading lamp, she sat listlessly on, an extraordinary indifference in her heart. The struggle was over for the time being; her wits were no longer stretched wellnigh beyond their limits, she gazed almost in panic through her glasses into a future empty and dull. The very essence of life had been dependent upon a neighbour's enmity.

It came to that, she thought, perceiving for a moment what a majesty of retort might still lie in Miss Pugh's simple withdrawal from the contest. The struggle had become foolish, sordid, profitless. How much better if she herself had kept aloof from even acknowledging the feud! How much easier had been her days if with perfect courtesy, and a crushing superiority, she had refused the battle her neighbour had offered. Her church, her parish work, her little social round—these would not then have suffered in the least. How many a sleepless night, how many a virulent pang of animosity would have been spared her! How much more dignified, and richer, her existence might have been if, with insufferable indifference, she had recognized her enemy only to ignore her importance.

Now, however, it was much too late. The fret was incessant; the Vicar had become a remote fruit of the Hesperides that a third and fleshlier antagonist would seize. Even her choicest acquaintances, and remote relatives, her friends, her sister were now banners and battlecries. She overheard herself positively parading them in talk with her visitors—talk meant to be overheard. Her garden that had once been her solace, her shrine of kindly remembrances —what was it now?—a mere imitative and ineffective effrontery to the next.

" 'Gardens!' " she thought with sudden disdain— when neither lady could afford more than one weekly visit from the same itinerant job-man; when neither could do else than deny herself the simplest of luxuries in order to purchase every expensive, listless, hideous and filth-devouring rarity the floriculturist might ordain. Like a dream of Vanity life seemed to her tired mind. "Only for a little peace!" she kept lamenting to herself. "Only to forget 'that' woman!"—who dealt with such magnificent ease almost intolerable blows.

"What will the creature do next?" she reminded herself: and at that the memory of her own insidious and secret triumph returned renewed. She rose and drew aside the blind to view that last most formidable retort. She perceived at the far end of the next garden Miss Pugh herself—feverishly planting by moonlight.

There was no need to watch. Intuition, poisonous as a serpent's tooth, had instantly whispered what deed she was at. "Unique" Rose for "Unique" Rose, cluster for cluster, would break into blossom alike, flaunting each its own lost novelty with every bud. Tit for tat! A Roland for an Oliver!—the foes were quits again; the great effort had proved abortive.

The elderly lady let fall the corner of the blind.

She turned with tears in her eyes, her heart a fiery coal of wrath and disappointment. So vehement and deadly was her rage that her cheek flushed scarlet at the thought which had zigzagged across her mind. "If it weren't for that interloper!..." She eyed herself hotly in the looking-glass, Cain answering to Cain.

Next morning she thought over matters more calmly. It was evident that a brief quiescence must follow this last effort. Tempted at first to uproot her rose tree then and there, she at last decided on the wiser course—to leave it apparently unconsidered, in hope that it might perhaps surpass expectation in its wealth and gaiety of bloom. Otherwise, she must return to the old doglike vigilance, ready to countervail without delay whatever tactics, whatever enterprise, her indefatigable and serene enemy might devise.

She was as usual compelled to toil on even to keep level. Weeding, pricking-out, pinching off, tying back, syringing, mulching, manuring—these were but a few of her laborious duties. The Parish, the Vicarage, the Guilds, the Teas, the Missions demanded each of them perpetual effort. With what ensuing *ennui* and surfeit only she herself could tell.

It was in an immense flood of light when the two rivals were next confronted. From stooping at their toil, they rose unexpectedly face to face across the dividing fence. Miss Pugh a little in the shadow of a dark tree, yet with spectacles brilliantly silvered; Miss Guthrie, petite, mousey, dowdy and insignificant in the full western blaze. Each bowed to the other curtly, frigidly, with a sneer in the extreme silence between them. Yet around them exulted the little earthly paradises of their own and of Nature's devising—smell, colour, sunshine, shade; the seemingly rapturous singing of their own refuges.

Almost involuntarily the two ladies turned away, and presently were busied as far apart as their fenced-in domains would admit.

But one eventuality was yet to appear; and upon its consummation Miss Guthrie's attention was now centred. To her amazement, almost to her awe, she made the discovery that of these two rarest of rose trees her own was certainly the more prosperous, vital and verdant. There seemed a youthful vigour even in its thorns that its rival lacked. Not yet languishing, perhaps, but surely beginning to cease to progress.

Miss Pugh stood there, shivering amid its luxuriant company. Buds it had in plenty, but flaccid, nid-nodding buds on blight-enfeebled stalks. *Was* it blight? Or an organic weakness? Or had Miss Pugh blundered?

Miss Guthrie narrowed her eyelids in derisive anticipation, and yet in perplexity. Miss Pugh had never failed yet. What kind of triumph then might this apparent failure predict? Hatred of her rival kindled anew at this instinctive testimony to her powers.

None the less Miss Guthrie covertly eyed the neighbouring garden, or squinnied down on it from

her bath-room window, a hardly believable symptom was everywhere revealing itself to her long-
practised eye—the signs of a brief neglect. Warnings
ignored by Isaac Watts's sluggard. Just that one
scarcely perceptible lapse from exactitude in everything that betokened a Nature stirring in her
bonds. She drew off her stiff and filthy gloves and
folded them together. A gush of malicious warmth
swept through her, wherein she suddenly perceived
that a bleak wind was blowing in the garden—a
wind absolutely impartial, absolutely indifferent.

She shot a quick speculative glance at Miss Pugh's
windows, displeased, she knew not why, at being
alone. What are flowers, their beauty passed away,
their sweetness gone? "Tell her that wastes her time
and me. . . ." She turned with a shrug of disgust
from their frailty, their useless loveliness, their
meaningless parade. She had no brains, never was
clever, she remembered. She could not puzzle the
problem out, nor evolve of herself what things in
her existence might ever be really always satisfac-
tory. If she could but find one unique object, set it
up beyond cavil and beyond reproach so that even
Miss Pugh must acknowledge defeat with honour.
Then? Why, then—her heart warmed to think how
friendly a body she herself could be; how pleasingly
apt to praise and flatter; how delightfully prone to
seek advice; while before, her every thought had
been acrimony and pretence.

There was no such talisman, however, to be found
by a tired and dull person. Industry, therefore, came

to her aid as usual, and the metallic din of her midget mowing machine sounded above the voice of the bird.

Next day Miss Pugh caught up again. The tall, large woman worked without a sigh from dawn to nightfall. And by then Nature, so far as she was concerned, was once more in exile. One thing only was beyond even genius; and strangely enough, and still as if she had some further overwhelming stratagem in her mind, she paid no heed to her last and latest rose tree—manifestly perishing. She passed it by with a broad rancorous smile almost audible—even to Miss Guthrie—once more peeping and peering from behind her curtains. She took no rest else, spent herself out, was a man in energy, a woman in ease and dexterity, and she returned by her back door in to her house at last with infinite slowness bearing her floral tribute, it's the spoils of all, their radiance reflected on her own flushed, damp brow.

Thereafter the days went by swiftly. Miss Pugh's bright grass rose up and flourished; her flowers (how gratefully!) faded unheeded to blessed seed. Caterpillar, snail and slug revelled unreproved. Greener than their foliage the greenfly swarmed into being—into generations—and ravaged the roses. And when, at last, Miss Guthrie's *Unique* broke all of a lovely gaiety to the sun, a budless skeleton, its brown leaves curled and tapping in her neighbour's garden, answered it again.

But Miss Guthrie, as she had in that one vivid moment in the past foreseen, found that only disaster lay in unmarked and unrecorded triumph. Her garden was become a burden to her; the new Vicar was more insipid than ever with no envious rival at hand to mark his affability. And beyond this, a strange and extraordinary uneasiness took possession of her.

Her disordered thoughts seemed to curtail themselves, only to give place to others as immature and untidy. She went about her chores like a person who has lost a thing invaluable and is ever inwardly on the alert to find it. For days together her charwoman flourished unreproved. She wished, with a strange anxiety, to *hear* of her neighbour. What was her malady, and when might she look for her return? For still it was this enemy, it was Miss Pugh, who was the only clear object in a mist of doubt and misgiving. Her head ached almost incessantly, and she would find her memory at a loss suddenly when most to be depended upon. She all but pined to be ill too; simply to have an excuse to give up, to surrender, to turn over a new leaf. And yet, stranger yet, only her garden, or rather Miss Pugh's garden, eased her care.

For there she might admire the lovely heedlessness of Nature and her ways. How casually the blooms clustered where the wind had come in the night; here where the linnet made ruin at rest with its singing. All grudge was gone, all malice was over now. Miss Pugh away, nothing seemed worth while, none great enough to continue the contest even in project. It was extraordinary, Miss Guthrie thought gloomily, how shallow had been her animosity against her; how poor a thing by contrast with this chill sense of solitude and fading laurels. She hid her eyes with her hand when she remembered her own homely face in the glass darkly, grotesquely transfigured.

With a sudden revulsion, she all but stripped her *Unique* of its blooms, and hastened indoors to tie them together for her neighbour, out of touch for so long with all such delights. But even when the flowers were ready, and the formal, childlike note had been written, she happened to think that perhaps even in illness that taciturn formidable soul might refuse her offering.

But there, what would it matter, she asked herself with shining eyes, if she *were* scorned and rejected, she would at least have made the attempt. Only, in case these particular flowers of all others might cause the anguish of resentment that Miss Guthrie herself knew so well, she changed her mind, put the roses in a bowl, and hatless, her gloves in her hand, opened the door with the intention of visiting the florist who at least might have *some* bloom, perhaps the flowers of a fruit far from the Dead Sea and all unforgivingness, which neither of the two gardens could show. She passed out, shut to her door and stood an instant at her gate, staring back, blank and cold, at her neighbour's windows. Were there really so many Venetian blinds to so few windows? Down, down, down, every one of them. And Miss Pugh dead, then!

Neighbours

She turned back into the house, ascending the steps with dry trembling lips. She stared at the purse already in her hand for the florist. She paused within the porch, in a miserable silence and uncertainty. The churchyard? the grave? No, she decided. If her secluded neighbour knew of her intent, she would prefer now—and without the least acrimony—to be left alone. Some day, perhaps, solely for her own sake, she would bring her a few wild flowers from her own now deserted garden.

THE PRINCESS

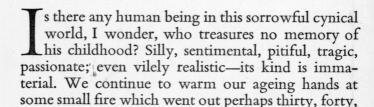

Is there any human being in this sorrowful cynical
world, I wonder, who treasures no memory of
his childhood? Silly, sentimental, pitiful, tragic,
passionate; even vilely realistic—its kind is imma-
terial. We continue to warm our ageing hands at
some small fire which went out perhaps thirty, forty,
sixty years ago!

Why? Because, I suppose, the experiences thus
hoarded concerned some silent very self—they were
rooted deep down, close in. . . .

Such an experience, for example, as falling in love;
and that not merely with a pretty face: but with, say,
a scene, a book, a character out of a story—yes, and
even with a phantom in a dream. Lord Byron had
his amorous adventures. But I doubt if he was ever
more truly, selflessly and faithfully in love than when
he was a boy of nine or so—and in love, and with a
child, too—Mary Duff.

He himself bragged about it in confessing it. He
even sneered at the episode and dismissed it scoffingly
as a childish amour. But he owned none the less that
the shock when he was sixteen on hearing that she

was married nearly threw him into convulsions. Convulsions!

Nor need any such infatuation be concerned with another *child*. A friend of mine once confided in me that when he was a boy not yet in his teens he used to spend hours loafing on an old brick wall hidden under the branches of a wild-cherry tree merely in hope of catching a glimpse of the fair-haired widow who lived near-by—a young woman of twenty-eight! Naturally, he "never *told* his love"—never, romantic imp, referred to the worm in the bud—until it didn't matter, and, too precocious in much the same degree, *he* didn't matter either, having become a juvenile roué.

The blossom of the wild cherry is as delicate as hoar frost, and as cool and beautiful as snow; but there is not much else to be said for it, nor for its tart hard berry, except possibly by the birds. And theirs seemingly are songs without words.

Well, I have a similar memory.

Like most children, I delighted in the old, fabulous fantastic stories—*Grimm's, Hans Andersen's*, the *Arabian Nights*. I loved old houses too, and particularly houses that appeared to be "haunted"—even if tales about them might send me shivering to bed.

And once, a lifetime ago, I managed to combine all these absurd fancies in one expedition. Not that it proved to be a triumph—even for *la belle Dame!* But for all that, memories, "silly" remembrances of this kind need not fade, or die, in our hands. Nor need they leave immitigable regrets behind them.

The Princess

At the time I am speaking of I can have been at the most only on the edge of my teens; and young too (as well perhaps as a little precocious) for my age. My mother had died when I was five, and after that I had been left pretty much to myself. We were living in Scotland, in Inverness-shire, in an old and rather ugly house. A desolate-looking scene stretched out beneath its windows, especially when one flattened one's nose against the glass and peered out on it through the frequent Scotch mists. But familiarity may breed affection. The house was only rented, alas! A lonely spot.

I had been at a loose end during those particular summer holidays, and had done badly in my school-work. To keep out of view of my father's challenging or aggrieved eye for as long as I could I used to rove about over the moors, indulging in fantastic day-dreams, and yet pining for company. In a mistified fashion too I was *looking* for something. There was a method in my meanderings. The something was a house, and the house had a story attached to it.

Not that at this time I actually knew its story. But the few crumbs of it which I had picked up by chance, in the kitchen, or while listening to the casual talk of my elders, had fed many a companionless hour. I had more than once even dreamed of the house, and at least believed that it was haunted. The word itself of course suggests old, solitary, and ruinous masses of unpruned ivy; owls, the banshee, a spectral moon in a scudding sky. Well, there was nothing of that in my head.

The Princess

On the contrary. . . . It was a Sunday morning in summer when I first chanced on the house, having yet again managed to evade kirk. There was no mistaking it. Its name was enwreathed in the foliations of its wrought-iron gates. It was a still and clear day, I remember; of a full but gentle sunshine. The house had a solitary and beautiful situation—hill and valley. At the back of it, and not a stone's-throw away, cascaded a mountain stream, full and deep after rain, and at all times with a natural fall of water upon rocks fifteen or twenty feet below. This fall made a low continuous musical roar, like that of jangling bells and voices. It reverberated the whole day long.

The house belonged, as I knew, to a princess, an Oriental princess, and therefore, as I supposed, a dusky one, from India, perhaps, Ceylon, Siam, somewhere in the East. (I hadn't realized that one might be just such a princess and yet—well, as pale as a narcissus—the *narcissus poeticus* even!) No board announced that the house was to be let. No temporary tenant, I understood, had ever rented it. Yet she herself, the princess, hadn't been near it for years. For how many years, I hadn't the faintest notion. Certainly it looked mute and vacant enough. A tragedy, a love tragedy, the story went, had exiled its owner. Faces had fallen glum, and tongues discreet, whenever I had heard it mentioned.

But putting two and two together, and making twenty-one of them, as a child will, I had come to the conclusion, (a) that my princess had been as lovely as the Queen of Sheba (and it was King Solo-

mon who was *wise*); (b) younger than this queen;
(c) that she had in her brief life always been
forlorn and solitary—a Mariana in a moated grange;
and (d) that she was dead! I was reluctant to be certain of this. And yet, she *must* be dead, I fancied, for
so only could I keep my romantic notions of her *safe*.
And yet in a foolish fashion, I hoped, *not*. On the
other hand, was not the house said to be haunted; so
couldn't I make the best of both worlds? You will
guess what I mean.

These ruminations, at any rate, had turned the
princess into a sort of dream-creature, all my own;
something ineffably lovely that only the young are
capable of creating, although it is the business of poets,
I suppose, to attempt it. And romantic? Well, isn't
that the only true meaning of the word? Indeed,
ridiculous though it may sound, in those greenhorn
days I too had fallen in love—sucking-calf-love—and
with a phantom!

Meanwhile, there I stood, steadily surveying the
house; fascinated, but a little repelled. Was it occupied? Most of the windows were shuttered; a few of
the upper ones were only curtained. Who and what,
I wondered, might not have taken up a lodging
here? There was a look of neglect, of the distraught,
but it was not extreme. Moss, damp, discolouration,
weather and season would account for much of that.
And you could tell at a glance that the place had
never been a happily peopled house; not at any rate
in recent years. In a word, it looked abandoned. And
the very effect of the air surrounding it changes

when a house had been abandoned. Humans are like that too.

There, in the shelter of a tree, I stood watching the house; drew nearer at length, paused under its porch, and listened. Not a whisper. Only the answer that silence gives. So I made my way to the back of the house; found a little unlatched green door; listened again, but could hear nothing except the noise of falling water and a faint shrill grasshopper-like trilling —like the twittering of birds, in the reeds and bushes of a stream.

Sunshine was pouring down; and, as for solitude, I might have been in the middle of the Desert of Gobi. I pushed the door gently inwards and took a look at the beyond. A stone-flagged passage evidently led into the kitchen quarters. I looked and listened—no clink of pan or clack of pot, no sizzling; not the faintest whiff of cooking on the air; only the mouldy and fusty. I ventured on. An old-fashioned meat-jack resembling the upper parts of a knight in armour stood in the kitchen. There was a gigantic table; heavy chairs, a gravy spoon, a rusty knife, and a stopped clock. No fire and a stopped clock! Well, anyhow, the cook was not at home!

Upstairs I stole at last, led onward by the phantom shape in my imagination; the dusky skin, the deep-memoried forlorn dark eyes. She haunted me; but my young fancy had done its best for her! At the end of a long corridor I came to a door ajar. All the rest had been shut. At this door I paused again. It had pretty coloured panels and a cut-glass handle. I looked

in. I even had the audacity to draw back a folding
shutter so that the sunshine should enter. No room I
had ever seen at that time resembled it; a low-
pitched moulded ceiling, deep, rich colours and em-
broideries, what I know now were Persian tiles and
dishes; and a few pictures, by the then unfashionable
French painters. Nothing Indian; no brazen god-
desses, tusks, elephant-pads, carved ivories, mother-
of-pearl. And no sound but those of the water—
hollow, musical, in a strange but enchanting tongue.

The room was a sort of boudoir, I fancied, and
nothing was amiss with it except only that the finest
dust faintly veiled the tables and obscured the glass.
And opposite the window in the sunlight there hung
on the wall a portrait. Whose, I knew instantly.
That the Princess of my imagination had been dark
and young and beautiful—there was nothing unlikely in that. But, except for no hint of duskiness in
the pallor of the cheek, how strangely close a re-
semblance was here! I myself might have painted
the portrait.

The forlorn dark eyes gazed steadily back at me,
sharing, or at least understanding, as it seemed, my
foolish boyish dreams. If a poem can be said to
resemble a quiet and lovely face, then this face
resembled a poem. It was suffused with its own
imaginations. How many leagues my astral body
flitted away at that moment I will not venture to
compute. A faint sound from below, scamper of
mouse or rat perhaps, recalled me to the predicament I should be in if I were caught. Well, I stole

away no less cautiously than I had come, and mentioned my discovery to not a single soul. . . .

More comforting than a ghost, I had seen the very image of the dreamed-of one. It was as if I had trespassed into some tale in the *Arabian Nights*—an abode of beauty and danger. *One* thing; I was no longer in doubt that my princess was dead. But Time, I was to learn, has other means of sepulture than the grave. . . .

It was winter and very cold when I came again to the house—an afternoon in January. Ice had diminished the roar of the waterfall, and there were no warblers now; only, among the hills, the crying of peewits. I approached the house from the back, this time from over the moor, an empty waste of virgin snow. There was a small winter sun burning clear in the sky, but with little heat—more like a lantern, and low towards the south. It had less than an hour to shine, I reckoned, before its setting. Splintery crystals of hoar frost shimmered on the green-blue paint of the door. It was even colder inside the house; and quiet as a tomb. Too quiet.

As if with the instinct of an animal, I suspected that this time I was not its only inmate. For a full two minutes I must have stood listening at the door of the room in the upper corridor. Yet at first glance within, all was well. The shutter lay open as I had left it; although now there was no direct sunshine—only on walls and ceiling a stark bleak unearthly brightness reflected from the snow.

The Princess

It will hardly be credited, but such was the folly of my young heart, that I had actually brought with me a bunch of early snowdrops; and, as it proved, I could hardly have made a less appropriate choice. In this cold bright silence I turned at once towards the portrait, as if for a welcome, and then, to my consternation, noticed that the door into the inner room was ajar.

I stole over to a window; and there, black as ink beneath it, stood drawn up to the porch a four-wheeled cab, the superannuated old horse between the shafts apparently asleep, and of a dirty yellowish white against the snow. I stared at it in dismay. And as I stood watching, there came a faint silken rustling, the whiff of an exotic scent, and, like a creature caught in a trap, I turned.

Pallid and painted, lean as a starving cat, and dressed up to the nines, stood in the doorway of the room beyond, the figure of a thin-nosed, haggard old woman, her black eyes fixed intently on me. In that spectral snow-light I was for an instant or two uncertain whether she was actual or an illusion. Motionless in her finery, with fixed sidelong head and starch-white face, she might have been a life-sized marionette, grotesque but intimidating. Besides, there are, in all of us, degrees of reality; and she appeared to have been "made up", in more senses than one. As to being an illusion she soon undeceived me. Nodding her head as she spoke, and in a voice resembling the jangling of strings in some old thumped-on, worn-out, schoolroom piano, she said:

The Princess

"How do you do? I fear you have had a cold welcome."

I made no reply. She then asked me who I was, and how I had found my way into the house. Mortally alarmed of her, I muttered my name and explained where I had come from. She then inquired what I had come *for*. And that for the moment stumped me.

"For what you can find, I suppose," she jeered. "Well, my young man, even magpies have tongues. Whatever else you may think covetable here, you won't discover anything to *eat*. That I can warrant."

Her old rouged sallow cheeks puckered up into a grin. She nodded at the snowdrops in my hand.

"What are those for?" she asked me.

The knowledge that in my embarrassment my face must have gone red as a beetroot only made me the more timid and disinclined to answer her. I said I had brought them for someone.

" 'Some one'? Some one *here*?" she retorted sharply. "Who? When?"

I turned a faltering head, glanced up at the portrait on the wall; and then, still speechless, fixed my eyes on herself again.

"For that?" she cried. "For *her*?" There was no mistaking her astonishment. "Well! And you expect me, my young gentleman, to believe it! Flowers for a picture! A pretty story—even if it is untrue. And who do you suppose that *is*?"

I had heard, I explained, of a princess who had once lived in the house. My father had talked of her, and the servants. The features of the jaded old face set into a stare and the black eyes seemed to pierce me to the marrow.

"A princess, eh? And what *kind* of a princess, may I ask?"

I told her that I thought she had come from the East.

"And gone *to*?"

"I supposed," I said, "that she was. . . ." Then I paused.

"Well? That she was? That she was—what?"

"Dead," I replied; and hung my head.

I cannot describe the precise change in her face at this announcement. Certainly no resentment showed in it. Indeed, for a moment its peevishness seemed to drain away out of it, and much, too, even of its age and its sardonicism. Another face, from out of the past, had been faintly disclosed. It seems strange that at that moment I did not realize whose.

"Oh, 'dead'," she repeated. "So the princess is dead? That's what they all say, is it? Convenient. But not much of a compliment, do you suppose? And what did you think this princess of yours would look like—well, if she *was* dead?" I ignored the sinister hint in the question, yet was momentarily fascinated by it. I merely nodded again towards the picture.

"Like that," I replied.

"Very naïve, and charming. Prettiness itself," she scoffed. "A secret assignation? But, if, my young stranger, the young lady was dead, who did you suppose was going to keep the tryst?"

The Princess

The old creature's eyes fixed themselves even a shade more intently on my silent face. "A ghost, I suppose? . . . So that's it?"

I shook my head, and had just enough courage to add, "I don't *think* I should have been frightened."

"Not frightened, eh?" she mocked me. "Not at a ghost? Quite a little Sir Galahad! And do you flatter yourself that you didn't look more than a little frightened when you saw *me*? Bless you, child, the bloom went out of your cheeks—like *that*. As if you had gulped down a dose of physic—castor oil. But perhaps you supposed that *I* was a ghost?"

There fell again a silence between us. Unless it were fancy, the waterfall had slightly changed its note. The frost, then, was deepening. The quiet lovely room was cold and still as a vault. I continued to gaze at my questioner, my hands clammy, my eyes like a bird's in the spell of a serpent.

"At first, perhaps, I did think you were a ghost," I managed to blurt out at last. "I wasn't sure *what* you were. Not at first. It startled me."

"*It*, eh? At *first*? But when you discovered that I was . . . well, flesh and—and bone, what then? You were still more frightened?"

"Oh, no," I lied; and added quickly to muffle the lie up, "except at being caught here."

"I see," she mocked meditatively. "And the snowdrops? Were they to be an offering to the paint, or to the spectre?"

Again I shook my head. "I was only going to leave them," I said.

71

"Quite a little romance! Train up the child in the way that he should go. Don't be alarmed. We all have to begin like that. But for the life of me I cannot make up my mind whether our little housebreaker is extremely backward for his age, or atrociously forward. How old *are* you?"

"Speak up," she said, when I had answered. "You need not be as frightened of me as all that. Perhaps you would like a pretty little vase for your posy and some nice cold water? Gracious heavens, try to come alive, boy! I could never abide day-dreamers."

By now I was ready to burst with misery, rage, and shame. And she saw it. Her face softened a little. "Well," she went on, "you can comfort yourself with one thing: I don't tell *tales*. I may resemble an old parrot; but I don't tell tales. Never did. I leave that to others." She had seated herself at the table.

"Come here and shake hands on it." The last of dusklight was beginning to drain out of the room; a paler, more furtive radiance was stealing in. I hesitated, went over, and held out my hand.

"God bless the boy," she cried, "has he *no* manners! I warrant now, if *that* young lady had been sitting here, you wouldn't have put out a lifeless paw to shake hands with. Not so much of a little Platonist as all that!" She had tugged off a needlework glove and had thrust out a blue-veined claw of a hand towards me. Its bony fingers were three deep with old rings. "There," she announced, "since I haven't a mince-pie or a slice of cake to offer you, taste that!"

The Princess

With infinite disinclination I did as she had bidden me, and kissed her cold lean hand.

"So you fancied your lady-love was dead—our innocent adorable nymph up there, of the sidelong look and downward glance! And now, boy, for a little secret. But this, mind you, is not for the servants!" She waited, staring at me, her head slightly trembling on her old shoulders. "Well, there are *two* kinds of ghosts. We may compare them to a nut. The one kind is the kernel. The other is the husk. At this moment you are contemplating the husk. Do I look it? Do I look that kind of ghost? Do I look—well, *dead*?"

God only knows I had never encountered a human being before that in some respects looked less dead, and yet so perilously near it. I turned my head away to hide the distress and aversion in my eyes; and then, such is childhood, I thrust the bunch of snowdrops into one pocket of my jacket, pulled out a dingy handkerchief from the other, and began to cry. The old woman waited until I had pushed back the handkerchief by faltering inches into my pocket again.

"There!" she said. "April showers. Happy dreams." And then she went on in a quavering, put-on, mocking voice, as though to deceive herself as much as me: "No, no, my child:

Nothing is here for tears, nothing to wail
Or knock the breast; no weakness, no contempt,
Dispraise, or blame, nothing but well and fair
And what can quiet us in . . ."

73

She paused again, and added in tones of an almost
metallic intensity yet trembling with derision,
" 'And what may quiet us in a death so noble.' So
you see I forgive you, and return you", she nodded
up at the portrait, "to your flawless and ingenuous
sweetheart. . . . You love her? . . . Yes? . . . Well, if
you cannot answer, don't. But next time, my bonnie
laddie," she glanced at my kilt and sporran, "fix
your heart on something a little more solid and un-
painted. Not of that *root*. . . . Meanwhile," her old
fingers had taken a key-ring out of her vanity bag,
"why not a little keepsake?"

She rose and unlocked a small Chinese cabinet
that stood against the wall behind her, and held out
to me in its opened case an oval miniature, sur-
rounded with garnets. I stared at it in the cold of the
moonlight; had no knowledge of its value or its
skill; but there was no mistaking the face of the
child there—a face that even a Leonardo might have
lingered over.

"This," she said, tapping her pointed finger-nail
on the glass, "this is where that", and she nodded up
at the portrait again, "came from. And this," she
made a wry mouth, tapped her breast and cast me
an ironical little bow, "*this* is where both went
to . . .; just for a while, you know—*Me*."

A remote gleam had come into the intense darkness of her eyes, else almost as motionless as the
burnt-out ashes of a fire.

"Now tell me", she went on, "if *that* had been
servants' gossip, if, before you set out house-break-

ing to-day, you had known what had become of your pretty lady-love up there, would you still have come, still have been here this evening? . . . Don't gawk, boy; answer me!"

I gazed at her, still hesitating between truth and cowardice, my eyes no doubt like a stricken dove's to-and-froing over her raddled face. And then at last I faintly shook my head. "No," I said. "Not if I had known." My lips were so dry that I could scarcely utter the words. "But wasn't she," I turned my cheek a little towards the picture; "wasn't *she* like that? Even *then*?"

The silence, the cold, the curious light, the solitude between us seemed to have intensified and the whole house to be listening. Then, "God bless my soul," the old woman cackled, "the boy's incorrigible! We should have met before. 'There would have been a time. . . .' There, put that bauble into your pocket before I think better of it; and go away. And next time, beware of man-traps!"

Her derisive face had hardened again. And at that, with some idiotic wish, I suppose, at the back of my mind to be quits, or possibly to make amends, I pulled my little bunch of snowdrops out of my pocket and held them out to her. She took them, sniffed greedily their earthy smell, looked at me, turned about, put them into the cabinet, and locked its door. And before she could say another word I had obeyed her, and was gone—out into the full wintry moonlight and the virgin loveliness of the snow.

THE GUARDIAN

There are, I am well aware, many excellent people in this world who shun anything in the nature of the tragic in connection with *children*. And particularly if it carries with it what they consider to be a strain of morbidity. My own conviction, none the less, is that childhood is a state of extremes; alike of happiness and of *un*happiness. And I speak from my own knowledge—derived from observation and experience long before this "psychiatry" became a craze—when I say, not only that some of the saddest, gravest, most dreadful and most profound experiences in life may occur in our earliest years, but that, *if* they do, the effects of them in after-life *persist*.

I am not a mother. I am what is called "an old maid"; but even "old maids", I assume, are entitled to their convictions.

I might first explain that I am the last of my family. In my earlier years I had three sisters. Philip was the only son—and a posthumous child—of the youngest of them—Rachel. And his mother was the only one of us to marry. What opportunities the others had to follow her example is nothing here to the point. At all events, they remained single. My sister's choice was a tragic one; her head was at the mercy of her heart. Her husband was a man who may be described in one word: he was wicked. He was selfish, malicious and vindictive, and the moment I saw him I warned my sister against him. But in vain. He failed even to contrive to die respectably. I mention this merely because his character may have some bearing on what I have to relate. But what, I can hardly say.

Philip was born three months after his father's death. In spite of the grief and affliction which my poor sister had endured during the brief period of her married life, there appeared to be nothing amiss with *him*. Nature goes her own way. He was a quiet and tractable child, although he was subject to occasional outbreaks of passion and naughtiness. He was what is called a winning little boy, and I loved him very dearly. He was small for his age and slenderly built. In his earlier years his hair, and he had a long and narrow head, was of a pale gold—straw-coloured in fact; but it darkened later to a pretty lightish brown, and was very fine. Hairdressers frequently remarked on this. He had a small nose, and deep-set but clear grey eyes of a colour seldom seen in company with *that* coloured hair. He looked delicate, but was in fact not so.

This appearance—and he was by nature a sensitive and solitary child—suggested effeminacy. But since in his case it implied only fineness and delicacy of mind as well as of body, it was nothing but a tribute to him. I consider it a poor compliment to a *woman*, at any rate, to be regarded as mannish and masculine. Let us all keep to what we *are* and as much of it as possible. On this account, however, I counselled his mother to send him to no school until he was in his ninth year. She herself was inclined to be indulgent. Still, I am a great believer in the influence of a good home-life on a young child. Affection is by no means always a flawless mentor; but I know no better. And as my sister, still a young woman, had been left badly off, I had the pleasure and privilege of paying for Philip's education.

I selected an excellent young governess with a *character*. She taught him, five mornings a week, and with ease, the usual elements; and I especially advised her to keep as far as possible to the *practical* side of things. His own nature and temperament would supply him with the romantic. And that I regarded with misgiving. Later, he was sent to what an old friend of mine assured me was a school—a preparatory school—where even a sensitive and difficult child might have at least every opportunity of doing well and of being happy.

His first reports—and I had myself insisted on being taken over the whole school, scullery to attics, and on having a few words *alone* with the matron—were completely promising. Indeed, in his third term, Philip won a prize for good conduct—a prize that in these days, I regret to hear, is disparaged, even sneered at. Not that rewards of this kind are necessarily an enduring advantage—even to the clever. Much depends, naturally, on what is meant by goodness.

Now, in my view, it is a mistake to screen and protect even a young child too closely. Mind; I say, *too* closely. I am no believer in cosseting. A child has to face life. For this he has been given his own defences and resources. Needless to add, I am not defending carelessness or stupidity. I remember seeing at a children's party a little girl in a flimsy muslin frock and pale blue ribbons—a pretty little creature, too—who exhibited every symptom of approaching measles. Shivery, languid, feverish, running at the eyes and nose—the usual thing: and I kept her by me and I warned her nurse. But it was too late. Thirteen children at that one small party eventually fell victims to this stupidity. As with risks to physical health, so with mental ailments and weaknesses.

Night fears and similar bogies may be introduced into a young and innocent mind by a silly nurse-maid or by too harsh a discipline, or perhaps by an obscure inheritance. They may also be *natural* weeds. When I was a girl, even I myself was not entirely immune from them. I dreaded company, for example; was shy of speaking my own mind, and of showing affection. I used both to despise and to envy the delicate —the demonstrative, and even on a summer's day was always least happy in the twilight. Least at home. The dark, on the other hand, had no terrors for me. As events proved, such fears not only affected Philip a good deal more than they affect most children, but with a peculiar difference. Indeed, I have never since encountered a similar case.

Towards the end of December in that year he came as usual to spend his Christmas holidays with me. This was an arrangement with which my sister willingly complied. But I had only suggested it; I never made demands. His trunk was taken up to his bedroom, and we sat down to tea, at which my cook, who had been many years in my service, provided for him a lightly-boiled egg—and I have never encountered even an old man who did not regard a boiled egg with his tea as a delicacy! As he sat facing me at the tea-table and in the full light of the lamp, I noticed at once that he looked more than usually pale. His face was even a little drawn and haggard. And "haggard" is hardly a word one would willingly use in relation to a child. But it is the right word. Moreover, his clear but wearied eyes were encircled with bluish, tell-tale shadows. *That* meant bad nights!

"You are not looking very well, Philip," I said. "You don't seem to be hungry after that long journey. What time do you go to bed? Do you have any supper? Are your lessons at school worrying you? Have you perhaps got into hot water with one of your masters? . . . No, I don't think *that*!" As far as I can remember, these were the harmless and unprying questions I put to him. Like most children, he made no attempt to answer them. I didn't expect him to; I intended to *glean*.

"Thank you, Auntie Caroline," he assured me

twice over, in his usual rather prim manner, for he was a demure little boy, and I object to *artificial* baby talk. "Thank you, Auntie Caroline," he said, "I feel very well. And I came out third or fourth in everything but French and Arithmetic. I was all but top in English." And then, after a pause, while I continued to smile at him, he added that at times he had not been *sleeping* very well. "I—often lie awake at night. And it goes on, you see, Auntie Caroline, sometimes into the day." Strange: I failed even to ask him what precisely he meant by that "it".

"Well, Philip," I said, "that I think we can easily remedy," although I had also failed to understand all the child may have meant by the words, *goes on*. "You must have plenty of fresh air in your bedroom, and a sufficiency of blankets: a glass of hot milk with a little water, and a biscuit for supper; and in case you happen to wake up, Pattie (my excellent parlour-maid) shall see that there is a night-light in your soap basin. Do you have a light in your bedroom at home?"

"Yes, Auntie," he said, "but not at school. And it's not a night-light. It's just a bead of gas. It's blue; and sometimes when I have woken up in the middle of the night, I thought it was an eye looking at me out of the dark. But, of course, it wasn't an eye. It was only a bead of gas."

"Well, it shall be a night-light," said I. "No one could mistake *that* for an eye, Philip?"

The next day at luncheon I thought he looked a little better. This, to be precise, was two days before

Christmas. It was our first day "Holidays Feast", as we used to call it; and luncheon consisted of roast chicken and vegetables, followed by a nice baked custard and some stewed prunes. In those days the small tart French prunes were still obtainable. Philip was exceedingly fond of bread sauce, and if it is not too richly flavoured, that is wholesome enough too. He steadily improved in looks during these holidays, and enjoyed his usual pantomime and one or two little Christmas parties. None the less, I noticed that whatever his spirits might be during the day, he became far less talkative at the approach of evening.

A little girl, the daughter of a neighbour whose name it is needless to mention, would sometimes come with her nurse to play with him. She was one of those apple-cheeked, nice-mannered, sensible little girls who in these times seem so rare. During the early afternoon the two children would be perfectly happy together; but towards nightfall, when the day began to droop, Philip's spirits would perceptibly languish. He would then only pretend to play, and at tea it was Rosie and I who talked; though I am sure that in her childish fashion she did her best to persuade him to come out of his shell and to smile again. But a child of seven who refuses to eat a slice of plum cake when he is neither ill nor homesick must be troubled in *mind* or already sick; I knew that and kept my eyes open; and presently the trouble came out.

When Rosie was gone, Philip took a picture book —a Christmas present—and sat down on a stool by the fire, while I resumed my knitting. A cautious glance or two at him soon revealed the fact that he had ceased to read, although his eyes remained fixed upon his book. With a sigh he would begin again: and yet again his attention would wander. That night I twice visited his bedroom. He lay quietly asleep, his night-light burning on the wash-stand. In the small hours I fancied I heard a cry. I listened, nothing followed; and I left my bedroom door ajar. Next morning, after breakfast, he trod by accident on my cat's tail. It proved to be a *fortunate* accident— at least, for Philip. Animal and child, they were on excellent terms with one another, but at the sudden exasperated squeal from the startled animal he was peculiarly affected, began to tremble, and suddenly burst into tears. Now *that* I regarded at once as an unmistakable symptom of nervous trouble. I waited until the table had been cleared, then I called him to me and said, "Philip, you must have had bad dreams last night. Pattie had not forgotten your night-light, I hope?" This, I am afraid, was a prevarication.

I see him now, in the holland overall which he always wore at meal-times and was then outgrowing, standing in front of me, his hand in mine, on the fur rug by the brass fender. A portrait of his maternal grandfather, whom he clearly resembled and who was not only a hard-working clergyman but a scholar, hung over the chimney-piece above his head. The light of the window—and it was a healthy, frosty, wintry morning—shone full upon his face.

"No, Auntie," he replied, "I had the light." But as he stood looking up at me I noticed that his eyes had begun to move away, as if involuntarily, towards the right, and that it was with an effort that he turned them towards *me* again; and then it was too late for him to suppress a faint expression of alarm on his pale, delicate features. What does this mean? thought I.

"Is anything frightening you now?" I inquired. Colour crept into his cheek, and a sob shook him. He nodded.

"In this very room?" said I, and searched with my glance the corner of it towards which he had turned. Nothing whatever was there that could account for his apprehension; no more unusual object, at any rate, than a bust of Cicero on its pedestal by the book-case—a precious possession of my dear father's. But with a child, one never knows.

"What's troubling you now?" I said. "Tell me, Philip." And I spoke in a quiet easy voice, gently fondling his small fingers.

"It's what, Aunt Caroline," he replied. "I see."

"See where?" I pressed him. "Look at the bright, sparkling garden—at the trees and the hoar-frost on their branches, thick almost as snow. Darkness, you know, Philip, can only remove that out of *view*. They themselves remain the same—no enemies there. Just as we two remain the same—light or no light. Is there perhaps anything troubling your *mind*? Look at Puss, now. He knows as well as I do that what happened just now was nothing but an accident."

"It's not in the *room*," he told me. "It's—it's inside. It's when I look right over—and turn my eyes this way, Auntie Caroline." They hardly wavered. "It began a long time ago; but—it's only sometimes."

"What is only sometimes?" I said. "At night, too?"

By dint of careful questioning, I discovered at length that what troubled him was no more, as I thought at the time, than a mere fancy. He told me that when he turned his eyes as far as their orbits admitted in a certain direction—and after recent experiments of this kind he had ventured to do this very seldom—he perceived a shape, a figure there. A something dark, small and stunted, I gathered, with humped shoulders and bent head, and steadily scrutinizing him. I was dismayed. Mere fancy or not, it was no wonder that a child so sensitive should be disturbed by so strange an unpleasant an experience as this, even if it were a pure illusion.

"Now tell me, Philip," I coaxed him. "Here we are, alone; just you and me. Aren't you perhaps imagining what you see? If we try, we can at once see your mother. In our minds, I mean. Can't we? But that too would be imaginary. And next moment she is gone. There *can* be nothing. Look again."

"Oh, Auntie!" he exclaimed, throwing his arms round my neck and bursting into tears again; "it's like that horrid, horrid Satan."

This, I confess, alarmed me, but I showed nothing of it.

"And who has been talking to you of Satan?" said I.

"Nobody, nobody," he cried passionately. "I saw it in a book."

"Ah!" said I. "Only in a book! Just a picture. That's where it comes from, then."

"Yes, Auntie," he sobbed, "*now*. But what I am telling you of was before that, *before* I saw it in a book."

I was intensely anxious to comfort the child, and assured him yet again that all this could be only fancy, that no more than a mere dream may haunt one's memory even in the full light of the day, that God protects the young, that the innocent have nothing to fear. And I took care to say no more than I believed. "Now, be brave. Just try," I said, "try once again."

"But you see, Auntie," he lamented, "it isn't always *there*. And oh! I can't. I daren't! ..."

Well, my very worthy family doctor came to see him. He declared the child was run down, highly strung, and so forth. That I knew. He prescribed Parrish's Food, and suggested, somewhat to my surprise, that he should be given half a glass of port wine every morning and afternoon. Still, when I ask for what I believe or have reason to hope will be good advice, I *take* it. And trusting that this treatment would soon mend matters, I refrained from writing to his mother. Matters did mend. We made no further reference, not the faintest, on either side, to what had troubled him. Not for some little time. Never reawaken trouble!

Little seemed amiss the following year. Philip

spent his tenth birthday with me, and then contrary
to my own conviction, but seeing how much better
and more confident he was looking, I asked him in
a jocular fashion, when his favourite pudding—a jam
roly-poly—was on the table, I asked him if he had
ever been troubled again with those old fancies of
his. He knew at once to what I was referring, and
met the question very gallantly, as I thought.

"Yes, I am now and then," he said, "but now I
never really look. He's *there*; but I think unless I
tried hard, I shouldn't see him. And at night—well,
you can't help what dreams come, can you, Auntie?"

But how different were voice, manner, air, by
comparison with the previous year. This being so,
it was on my lips to counsel him to make the
attempt then and there. Also to tell him of a mysterious belief in what are known as guardian angels.
But—although I have no wish to be uncharitable—
few even of those of us who share this belief *seem* to
pay any active heed to it, and in the fear that he
might perhaps be laughed at on this account at
school, I refrained. The adult, alas, is not always
courageous enough concerning his convictions on
behalf of childhood.

"Well!" I said. "We all have our little troubles,
Philip, and we must do our best to learn to face
them." He smiled at me. We understood one another. "Pattie," I said, "give Master Philip another
slice of that excellent pudding."

On reflection, it astonishes me that it never at any
time occurred to me to consult an oculist. That

might at once have put things right. Even people of excellent commonsense may occasionally be the prey of illusions—ghosts and similar nonsense. Charles Wesley, for example. And how easy it is, on a slight pretext, to give shape and meaning to what is purely the work of fancy. Hasn't the famous poet Shakespeare a passage in one of his plays concerning "airy nothings" or some such words? Even the best, the most skilful of oculists—and I should have chosen a good one—might very well have ascribed the child's fancies to a disordered liver, to those floating specks we may observe when we look at a white-washed ceiling. As for many of these mental specialists who are so much in evidence nowadays, I have, I confess, very little patience with them, or belief in them. Again perhaps I am wrong. But tampering with a child's mind is a dangerous experiment; and if it is put in the wrong hands, it may prove as clumsy an operation as that of a schoolboy using a penknife to repair his watch. And it will have much the same result.

There is one small thing I ought to add. I had discovered that this figure, this skulking shape, which Philip professed to "see" at certain times, was not always *stationary*. Also, that the hump at the shoulders *appeared* to be that of folded wings which, on one occasion at least, he told me, were lifted (like a raven's or a vulture's); as we see in Gustave Doré's illustrations to the poet Milton's *Paradise Lost*; or is it Dante? But there again, a picture no doubt accounted for this.

The Guardian

The following year Philip did admirably at school. He had one illness from which he completely recovered. He still *looked* none too robust, but this was merely "looking". He was a thoroughly nice, straightforward, pleasant English boy, not easy at making friends, but able to make good ones; which is all the battle. And I am thankful to say that he seemed to have inherited no adverse characteristics from his father. None the less, all my confidence, all my hopes for him—and words could not express my feelings even now, so many years after what followed—were doomed to be shattered.

A few weeks after his twelfth birthday, June 7th, I received a telegram from his headmaster. Only six words, which shocked me more than I can say: "Please come at once. Grave illness." "Grave"; that one word was enough. When, within twenty-four hours of the receipt of this message, I arrived at the school and was at once closeted with the headmaster, he told me, to my consternation, that Philip, two nights before, had made an attempt to run away.

"To run away?" I repeated, blindly, eyeing my informant. "Philip? Why? Where to?"

I could see by one or two little signs that in spite of his restrained manner and carefully chosen words, he—the headmaster, Mr. Morgan, I mean—had been shaken by what had occurred. And I had no intention of being unjust. I was merely seeking the *facts*. Indeed, a few such questions soon made it clear to me that this statement was not precisely in *accord-*

ance with the facts. That Philip had intended to make this attempt there seemed to be little doubt, since an old discarded rope from the gymnasium had been discovered hidden away behind his Sunday clothes in his locker.

What seems actually to have happened was this. For reasons unknown, the poor boy had recently been neglectful of his school work. Nothing more serious than inattention and a tendency to absent-mindedness—to day-dreaming. That far-away look in the eyes which I knew so well. He had got into trouble, too, for leaving food on his plate. Loss of appetite, I suggested. On the other hand, there had been no hint of positive unhappiness, and certainly not of deliberate wrong-doing. Nor, it seems, had he confided what he intended to do to any living soul in the school, not even to his closest friend or chum, a freckled, honest-looking boy named Ollitt.

On the previous Tuesday, none the less, a few minutes before midnight, without awakening or disturbing any one of the four boys who shared his dormitory with him, he must have risen from his bed, opened the window, and crept out on to the narrow ledge of stone beyond it. It was, as I remember myself, a quiet and lovely night, the more serene for its moonlight. No rope had been used; that was certain. That had remained in his locker. "If he had been awake—even partially awake," I argued silently, "why no rope?" The headmaster continued to look at me, but we found no words to express our feelings.

The Guardian

My own conviction—and I see no reason to change it now—is that, aroused, perhaps by some evil dream, Philip had been "walking" in his sleep. There was no breath of wind that night—nothing that could have alarmed the poor boy. And yet, the vivid moonlight, perhaps an inward realization of danger, something must have broken in on his sleeping mind, and aroused him—and then, no doubt, a frantic and desperate struggle to climb back into safety again. But in vain. The child, only, please God, half-conscious of his surroundings, and still under the influence of his dreams, had fallen headlong on to the flagstone path beneath the dormitory window. Within a few minutes he had been found there, unconscious, terribly injured. How little hope there was of his recovery was revealed by the headmaster's face as we sat together, both of us fallen silent again. He himself was in no way to blame; no one was to blame; and without hesitation I then and there said so. . . .

I was taken into the sick-room—a whitewashed, cheerful, sunny room. There was a glass of flowers on the table—pinks, I remember. The room contained five beds. Beside the furthermost of them, to the right of the other doorway and in a little cubicle, a dormitory maid was sitting—the matron herself having left the room only a few minutes before. She appeared to be reading to herself, with lowered head, from a book. She was a pale-faced little thing, looking younger than I learned she actually was—with her fair straight hair, and quiet, grey eyes. Indeed, she was little more than a child. At sight of me, she shut her book, rose from her chair, curtsied—a thing seldom seen nowadays from girls of any class —and left the room.

My dear boy lay on his back, mercifully out of pain for a while. He was tranquil, seemed to be asleep, or on the verge of being so. I sat down in the vacant chair and watched him. But that afternoon I had no word with him. During the next morning, he was in charge of the trained nurse that had been sent for. But I was allowed to sit with him again immediately after luncheon. His mother could not arrive until the next day. And then, it was feared, she would be too late. He had not heard me cross the room and slip quietly into the chair beside his bed. He lay with closed eyes, deathly pale, his head moving restlessly on his pillow. And as with sickened heart I sat watching him, his lips began to mutter, and the eyeballs beneath the closed lids to waver.

Whether he was sleeping or waking there was only one interpretation of the expression—sorrow, and, as I fancied, fear. I could not bear to see it. "Philip," I whispered, stooping over him. His features instantly became motionless.

Otherwise there was no sign that he had heard. He was listening; caught up, it seemed, by some acute expectation. The grey eyes slowly opened and met my own. It was too late. The faint smile of welcome with which he now greeted me could not efface the darting piercing disappointment that had first been revealed in their depths. "Dearest Auntie

Caroline," he whispered after a moment's pause, putting out his hand to me. "Am I very ill?"

I smiled again, and bent and kissed the bloodless fingers. "There, my dear," I said. "Lie quietly; all will be well. And there is no need in the world to say anything unless you wish."

The doctor himself had warned us that the boy was not to be crossed in anything. And I realized what that meant. In the brief, broken talk between us that followed, he confessed that he had some days before made up his mind to run away. To his mother I admit, not to me; and then he had decided otherwise.

"Why, Philip? What had made you so unhappy?" I ventured.

"*Not* unhappy," he assured me. "I was too happy. But—but, you see, it was no use. It never *could* be."

This completely perplexed me. But how ask a child why he is *happy*! "Then there was nothing—I was with you a while when you were asleep, my dear—there was nothing on your mind; nothing to be afraid of?"

Yet again the eyes turned restlessly in their sockets. "Afraid, Auntie!" he said. "Oh, no. I don't mind *that* now. Nothing to be afraid of now, I mean. It's still there; but now—it doesn't matter." And what I saw in his face at this moment was certainly neither dread, nor terror, nor even misgiving, nothing of that—but a grieved, profound, unutterable longing and pining.

"Listen, Philip," I said; "your mother will soon be here, very soon."

"That's lovely," he replied. But to my consternation—since I can truthfully say I had never in act or thought stood between them—there was *something* —a tone, an accent—wanting even in that "lovely", however sincerely it was meant. What then else could he be pining for? What could I do—or say— to rest his mind, comfort him? I pondered in vain.

The plain whitewashed room was radiant with light. It was a beautiful summer morning; the airs at the window ebbed in, sweet with the flowers of the garden and the smell of new-mown hay. Out of the distance came the noise, the voices, of the boys in the playing-fields. . . . A day of darkness, leaden clouds and pelting rain would have been easier to endure. At that time I had already steeled myself to many things in this world; but a life, I can truthfully declare, was slipping away far from me more precious than my own. I was a stranger to all this. I had never, except once before, felt helpless and forsaken. But how console a child with *that*!

And then, as if in direct answer to the question, the fallen narrow face on the pillow had suddenly become still again. The eyes beneath the leaden lids had moved to their extreme angle—away from me. And this, at the sound of a footstep. The door opened; I looked up.

It was the little dormitory maid. She had come to tell me that my sister had arrived, and would I join her in the headmaster's study. I looked at her—her face vaguely recalled some old picture I had seen. It was a quiet face, not pretty, but fair, with an unspoilt, remote look in her eyes. For an instant I could not reveal my thoughts. I was intensely reluctant to go. I smiled at her as best I could. "Then I can commit my nephew safely to *you* for a few moments?" I said.

She turned to look at him—as I did. And—how describe what I saw? There was no expectation now, no foreboding, or pining in the face on the pillow. No trace of these. But a look fixed on her as near human ecstasy as mortal features are capable of. I detest anything even resembling sentimentality; but my heart seemed to clap-to in my body. No expression on any human countenance, not even of hopeless grief or anguish, has ever affected me so acutely. Nor had I realized until that tragic moment —nor have I ever either more than once shared—its inward meaning. But there was not the least doubt of it. The poor child was in love.

THE FACE

Nora sat on the edge of her iron bedstead, the fingers of one hand firmly grasping the rail, her two strong legs, set wide apart, half-supporting her as she gazed out of the window. The eyes under the dark brows in her square, strong-boned face were vague with reverie; aware —yet heedless—of all that was happening in the neat rectangular back gardens down below.

It was two o'clock, and a Sunday afternoon. The leisurely September sun was now slanting fiercely towards the west. Its beams shone through the yellow and red of the canary-creeper and the nasturtiums along the garden fence, as if their flowers were of frailest coloured glass. And the panes in the gay, green-and-white little greenhouse at the foot of George Trimmins's garden flashed so like a heliograph that the face up at the window shone in its reflected light—like the moon's.

Mrs. Trimmins, his mother—voluminous body, large grey head—having now gone indoors, no doubt for her Sunday nap, George was sitting in his shirt-sleeves among his pigeons; snow-white creat-

ures that tooralooed and paced and ducketed on the
gravel about his feet, while two of their fellows cooed
love secrets into his ear. Across a white wing, he
would ever and again cast up furtive glances at the
open window. But Nora just now wasn't thinking of
him. She was trying to make up her mind whether to
set off at once for "the Ponds" or—not to. She
knew that everything would be bound to look different. She realized that, in spite of its vividness, the
memory of the night before might seem little more
than an illusion in the light of day—and that of a
Sunday afternoon! But she must chance it. She had
even now and then positively *hoped*, though her lips
tightened a little at this, that it would.

Either way, it would be better to have it over and
done with. In some respects the whole experience
had been so absurd, so ridiculous, and fantastic, so
unlike her usual, common-sensical self. What indeed
can it have had to *do* with her? And how could it
possibly have made such a difference? Still, even if it
had done so—just for the time being—what did it
matter? Except—well, would she ever be able to explain it even to herself?

That was the worst of it. There was no positive
need, of course, to tell anyone else a word about it.
But George? She would have to tell George. Exactly what? How much? He might understand the
solitary walk—the wish, almost the craving to be
alone. He might think her silly—daft, if you like; so
far. But what about the face which she could still see,
even with her eyes as wide open as they were open

now and fixed on his pacing pigeons—that was the absurdest thing of all? How could George possibly ever be made to understand *that*.

The decision would have to wait for a while, until they were alone again. But how was she to sit through the evening that was coming as if nothing had happened? Never before in all her born days had Nora's mind been so full of thoughts that wouldn't stay straight, that wouldn't match, that wouldn't let her out. What could be wrong, what had come over her, and when was she going to become her usual, matter-of-fact self again? Hands, like her mother's, square and capable, but now idle in her lap; her bosom slowly heaving as she drew breath her thoughts at length drooped back into day-dreaming again, and as if into the company of another self. Then suddenly, with a sigh as deep as water from a well, she withdrew her gaze from the window, floated up out of her reverie, and here she was, back in her small, square bedroom again!

Illuminated texts hung from unnecessarily large nails against the faded, damp-stained, blue-patterned wallpaper: "Thou Searchest Out All My Ways", above the grained washing-stand, and over the mantelpiece, "The Price of Wisdom is Above Rubies": its "price" in pale green, its "wisdom" in clear blue, and its "rubies" a rich red. Nora, from the time when she was a little girl of five or six, had explored every fraction of every inch of these texts again and again. She knew by heart every single one of the wooden-looking doves in the first; every sea-shell and fragment of sea-weed in the other.

On the mantelpiece itself were arranged her china animals; "quaint" hideous treasured creatures, some with large bows of ribbon round their necks. They were one and all eyeing her with a vacuous grin combined with an incredibly void stare. And in between them stood photographs of bygone "boys". One of them in a hard straw hat, leaning nonchalantly against a property urn; another, with his brother, seated on the steps of a bathing-machine in marine surroundings; and the same young man, now topped with what appeared to be a rococo paper nightcap, and evidently the "life and soul" of an animated and well-bottled group in an open charabanc.

On the chest of drawers Nora's father, Mr. Hopper, faced Nora's mother. He, as usual, was gazing blandly out of the cardboard at his daughter; and her mother sitting there, ample yet solid, was staring no less flatly across in his direction, as if at the moment she had far from approved either of him or of the photographer. However, there she *was*, and who cared who saw her! Nora took after them both. She had her mother's compact square head, frank challenging eye, and full figure; and yet, even at this moment, a glimpse of her father's half-wistful reserve lurked somewhere in her young vigorous features.

Of George, there was no trace in the little room. Although Nora had been engaged to him for weeks now, his photograph was still shut up in a drawer.

The Face

Why, she hardly knew. She didn't mind Alf and Sidney watching her dressing and undressing out of their skimpy little frames. They had nothing to do with it. Why George, then? He was coming this evening to Sunday supper; to be introduced to Uncle Ben and Aunt Emma. Nora shifted uneasily. She recalled other family reunions. She hadn't forgotten the evening when her Uncle Joseph, who had finally emigrated to Australia, brought his wife and children to see them. Nor her own Confirmation either! But Mrs. Hopper had known George and his family for years; from when he was a little boy, his hair smarmed down with hair oil, and his small square snubby nose in the middle of his face. He and Nora were going to be married.

She looked up sharply, rose to her feet, her mind made up. She would set off to "the Ponds" at once. Her father was safe downstairs in his easy-chair, his handkerchief over his head. It was the one thing he couldn't abide—flies. And her mother in the next room for the time being at least, must be far beyond all interest in Nora's doings—her patchwork quilt half drawn up over her petticoats, the rest of her completely *negligé*.

Nora's sudden hasty activity, however, had not been entirely unheeded. Her fiancé had at last realized that the young lady up above wasn't concerned just now with him and his "fancy". He wasn't hurt; no fear: she had her moods and her silences. Pretending not to have been even hoping,

The Face

he clapped his hands, and Nora watched from under the brim of the hat she was putting on before her looking-glass as—with a sudden drumming flutter and scurry—away went the beautiful birds up into the vacant heavens, their wings, cold and white as drifted snow, clapping together under the blue of the sky beneath the furious gaze of the sun. They gathered, they circled, they returned—as they always returned; back to their little pagoda-like dove-cote, back to Mr. Trimmins's sleek green-and-white greenhouse with its ripening tomatoes.

Her hatpin between her teeth, Nora decided that he really was a good sensible sort—that young Mr. Trimmins, in spite of his being such a sobersides and in spite of the interest and time he lavished on his almost uncanny knack with pigeons and tomatoes.

She pushed home the pin, and in a few moments had slipped out into the blinding afternoon. The street was deserted. Its opposite row of yellow brick houses sat roasting in the sun, as if they had been hollowed out of one lump of clay and now were crisp and finished. Someone was playing a hymn on a harmonium. The sound of it intensified the heat fourfold. But Nora didn't mind the heat. She loved it. Yet still, as she hastened on, with a steady clack-clack-clack of her best shoe-heels on the glinting flagstones, something in her mind was doing its utmost to persuade her to turn back. But no; those full red lips closed more firmly; the sensible thing to do was to face things out. And on she went.

The Face

At the end of the next street she boarded a tram, and edged herself in on to the hole-patterned seat immediately facing a family of Sunday merry-makers—the father (with his little dark moustache), the mother (her ringed left hand pressed close against the bag she carried), and their three small children in a row beside them—six, four, and two— with completely motionless bodies, and unceasingly active red-brown eyes.

It was stuffy in the tram. Nora watched the stagnant shut-up shops slide by—the butcher's, the draper's, the dairy, the fried-fish shop. *The Admiral Napier*—with its chipped padlocked brown doors— suggested a frivolous attempt at disguising itself as a morgue; its upper paint a leprous grey. The confectioners' were open, though; and so were the tobacconists'. She could see the boys, squatting on stools in their Sunday clothes, eating ices; and Mr. Jobson in his shirt-sleeves leaning over the last of his Sunday newspapers, smoking one of his own minute black cigars. "Triple murder in Kensal Green. Blood-stained chopper found." "Well-known Peer charged with Bigamy." The placards were always exciting on Sundays. Nora's gliding dark-blue eyes snatched at their novelties as the tram in its steel grooves lurched on. It was the world she was used to and it intensely interested her.

But when at length she reached "the Ponds"— their shelving banks shaded with lofty, bowering willows, green and silver in the motionless sunlit air

—they were all but deserted. At this first glimpse of them again Nora sighed. Just that one deep draught of sweeter air that had filled her lungs, had stilled her mind, set her heart beating. Her dark eyes had become almost as placid and absent as her father's. The water lay there, unruffled by even the faintest motion of the air, and blue as a plate beneath the sky. On the farther bank, but so far away that their shrill voices sounded not much louder than starlings', a swarm of small boys were disporting themselves; some shying stones into the water, while two or three of them were drying themselves in the sun—small, lean creatures, standing mother-naked under the bowl of the sky on the warm green turf.

And Nora at length softly turned her eyes towards her tree. This, too, was a willow, but it was a good many years older than most of its companions, and in part devoured and hollowed by rot. It leaned far out over the water from its few feet of grass-green sandy bank. And, as she looked at it, the complete experience of the night before flooded back into memory.

It wasn't as if that had been her first nocturnal visit. This, indeed, was one of Nora's own few secret resorts. She was "friends" with the place. She had paddled in its shallows with her school-mates, when quite a little girl. She knew its dangers; had been warned of them again and again. How then could she have been so stupid, so idiotic? To have stooped there remotely day-dreaming in that quiet starry darkness, leaning so far out over the water, with the perfectly ridiculous intention of trying to see her face in that dark mirror. The folly of it! As if to bid it good-bye! It would have served her right to have fallen in for good and all. What actually *had* happened—nothing so tragic—had happened in the twinkling of an eye.

Either in sheer absent-mindedness, or because she had been startled suddenly by the squawking of a little owl in the branches over her head, her fingers had slipped, and in she had gone. Down, down—like a stone, into the cold, greedy, caressing water. And, in an instant or two, though it had seemed an age, and an age crammed with a wild incoherent disturbing dream, she had come up again, panting, terrified, clutching; trembling, shuddering, but safe.

Better to have drowned almost than to have proved oneself such a silly! But it was then—as if it were hovering in the darkness of the air—that that strange phantom face had appeared. She had found herself gazing straight up into it; though whether, with the water streaming from her hair, her eyes were open or shut, she could not remember. It was through those few everlasting moments the face had stayed there, lit faintly as if by some light of its own, smiling, seraphic, unchanging, the eyes faintly luminous, the cheek narrowing softly to the chin, the hair drawn gently backward from the brows.

At length, and none too easily, Nora had pulled herself out, up on to the bank, had sat there, exhausted a while, to recover her breath, her safety, and her wits. And then, having wrung some of the water out of her clothes, she had hurried off home by as obscure a route as she knew, and so up to her bedroom. Her mother had been ironing in the kitchen when she left home. One of the flat-irons still sat cooling on the scorch-patterned ironing-sheet beside its holder. Nora had glanced at it as she came in. And like everything else in the kitchen, it seemed to be in collusion with her—and to be professing it! "*We* know; it's over now; don't be afraid. *We* shan't split!"

None the less Mrs. Hopper's sharp eyes had instantly noticed the change of clothes. "I thought you said George wasn't coming to-night? You haven't put a plate for him."

And Nora, without a word, had gone to the dresser to fetch one.

Why had she prevaricated? What was there to conceal? She didn't mind her mother. Why hadn't she confessed straight out that like a fool she had fallen into the water, and had had the sense to change her clothes? To tell the truth was as much a habit with her as to wash her face in the morning and to do her hair. Yet she had looked back at her mother, as if she had been accustomed to telling lies all her life—lies shameless, brazen. Yet even while she did so, she had been perfectly conscious of that faintly outlined face still haunting senses, memory, heart and mind. And it seemed to have no more connection with her mother, no more connection with telling the truth, and with living one's ordinary life than—well, Nora had no comparison.

A young man and a young woman were now straying hand in hand aimlessly and vacantly in her direction along the bank of the Pond. The three small boys were squatting on the green grass in their shirts. The sun had descended a little in its narrowing autumnal arc. Nora, after yet another fleeting half-glance at the scene spread out before her, turned back and hastened home.

Sunday tea was never a talkative meal. Unlike her husband, Mrs. Hopper was a heavy sleeper after meals, and—her Sabbath afternoon hour over—she invariably stumped down from her bedroom, cross, flushed and staring, and with sleep-glazed eyes, like a gently gaping fish. This afternoon, the meal was briefer than usual. There was High Tea or Early Supper to get. And Uncle Ben had a critical eye and a fastidious palate. But there's nothing like getting busy and working hard at whatever comes next, to prevent one's mind from brooding on what one is trying not to remember. Nora even sang over the peeling of the potatoes, and Mrs. Hopper wondered, on hearing her, why when she herself was young, she had been so squeamish, so strait-laced. Alf had been a good husband as husbands go, but there are all kinds of men.

In spite of her mother's rather cantankerous snort at the arrangement, Nora seated herself between her

The Face

father and Aunt Emma at the supper-table. But Mrs. Hopper was a woman as easily placated as she was put out; and her hospitality was second-nature to her. "There's Elf, now," she would explain. "He can't be anywhere but he's alone. He can't be anywhere but cooped up in his shell. Not me! Give me faces; give me company; give me *talk*. I'd mope me head off with nobody to see."

There was no doubt of it. The dark round table, with its cold boiled leg of mutton, its steak-and-kidney pie, pickles and beetroot, and glass and cutlery, and the china lamp in the middle, was packed as close with humanity as chairs would allow. They might be animals colloguing together. Yet Mr. Hopper merely sat quietly smiling there, and looking as much alone as if he were an ascetic Robinson Crusoe on his desert island.

Uncle Ben, however, having assured himself that his sister-in-law hadn't forgotten his distaste for bottled beer and his "pongshong" for whisky, had lost no chance to keep up his reputation as a wag, and a lady-killer. And, with Aunt Emma for flattering ally, and Miss Mullings, as a new victim so far as he was concerned—sidling but appreciative—for audience, there was soon an unceasing roar of talk and laughter. And as naturally as flies round a chandelier, it had circled about the guest of the evening—the doomed bachelor, the greenhorn of matrimony, the wise-crack's easiest cockshy—George. George was solid; George was a stayer; a bit thick-headed, if you like, but none the worse for that perhaps when life wields so clumsy a club and cracks a sensitive skull as easily as a steam-hammer cracks eggs. George was *there*; to bear the brunt, to play the butt, the future bridegroom! And George, in his tight starched collar and "neat" pepper-and-salt suit, had met every sally with unfailing good-humour, even though, with his head bent forward a little and his dark brown eyes slightly bulging, he resembled the while a bullock staring out of a cattle-truck.

Uncle Ben had the richest stock of jokes for all occasions—from a christening to a funeral. But his marrowiest were on the subject of widows, mothers-in-law, and young people in love.

"Lor', now, Ben," Mrs. Hopper had come to the rescue at last, "give him a chance; give him a chance!" With a hiccup of ribald amusement and a sigh of exhaustion, she wiped away the tears from her eyes.

"Chance!" retorted Uncle Ben, turning his long nose in her direction. "What's he want with chances? Hasn't he had his chance, and hasn't he taken it? . . . And won't he?"

George shifted an inch or two on his chair.

"He don't want no chances." Aunt Em intervened, drawing her hand across her mouth. "He's happy enough, *I* can see, and so would any young man be."

"What I say is," said Uncle Ben, with extraordinary solemnity and almost squinting at his friends, from eyes that were, even at ordinary moments, formidably close together, "what I say *is*, he's joined the old redoubtables. He's taken the plunge—and come up smiling." He looked firmly at the tumbler in his hand.

"Anybody, to hear that, Mr. Hopper," Miss Mullings insinuated, "would suppose that a journey to the altar was no better than a young couple going to their execution."

"Altar, did you say, Miss Mullings, or halter?" inquired Uncle Ben punctiliously. "And what, might I ask you, does anybody expect at an execution? Why, to lose his head! Aye, and to have it picked up out of the sawdust before the trickling lids are down over the eyes. When I think of our young friends on that track—well, there—" his voice sank into a plangent whisper and he emptied his glass, "my heart bleeds for them."

"Pull the long bow, you do," Mrs. Hopper expostulated. "Why, if it wasn't telling secrets, I recollect a time, Ben, when you as near as possible fell into the trap yourself; and a nice plump young widow, too, though I'm not too sure all that hair was her own!".

Mr. Hopper, who had been steadily and quietly eating the while, at this, gently slid his eyes in his brother's direction, and smiled. It was like a watery glint of sunlight in a raining sky.

"That", retorted Uncle Ben imperturbably, "is what might look to be a bulls-eye. But, 'twice shy' is my rendering of it. I read the other day, in an old book I came across, of two islands out in the East there, three hundred miles apart. Two islands: one

inhabited by nothing but men, and the other by—
well, in short—women. So I know where I'*m* going
to when I die."

"But which, Mr. Hopper?" murmured Miss
Mullings.

Uncle Ben threw up his two knuckly hands.
"*Kamerad! Kamerad!*" he cried. "Now George,
here . . ." he began again.

George pushed his chin a little further over his stiff
collar; and swallowed.

"There's some of us not so easily taken in," he
muttered thickly. "What *I* say is, the proof of the
pudding is in the eating."

The worm had turned, but at the sound of his
voice, Nora had begun hastily collecting the dirty
plates together in preparation for the plum tart and
custard and a plum-pudding that Mrs. Hopper,
since the Christmas before, had faithfully reserved
for whatever occasion Providence might propose.

And it was not until after the supper dishes had
been cleared away, and Uncle Ben—who didn't
think even as much as small beer of "all this Voder-
veal"—had entertained the company with a few out
of his familiar repertory of songs, that the attention
of the little party suddenly centred itself on Nora.
From her brief solitude in the scullery she had slipped
back into the room again and seated herself beside
her father. His hand had crept out and gently
clasped her own for a moment, where it lay in her
lap, palm upwards, on her knee.

The Face

Aunt Emma, at the same moment, with a curious, crab-like movement, had slipped from her stool at the old rose-wood, silk-pleated piano, and Uncle Ben, whose third song had not been received with precisely the volume of applause to which he was accustomed, had observed this furtive little caress.

"Now, if I was a goose," he cried gallantly, "there's one young lady present which I don't believe could say 'Bo' to me no how. What do *you* think, pretty Miss Pensive, now, with them dark eyes?"

Mrs. Hopper who, up to this moment, had seemed to be completely unaware of her daughter's small share in the evening's entertainment, suddenly lost patience.

"God's sake! She's sat there, dumb as an image, all the blessed evening. What's wrong with you, girl?"

At this, George's eyes, which had been as steadily fixed on his beloved as a bullock's in a truck on a drift of green pasture at the railroad's edge, turned heavily away, while a dull red mounted up into his naturally dusky face.

"*I'm* all right, Mother," said Nora.

She was alone in the world again; for at first sound of Mrs. Hopper's rebuke, Mr. Hopper had withdrawn his hand.

"If you was 'all right' as you call it," retorted Mrs. Hopper, "you'd prove you had a tongue in your head. She's been like this for days together," she explained to Aunt Emma. "I can't think what's come over the child."

The Face

"Maybe she's not feeling quite the thing," Miss Mullings suggested sympathetically.

"Now then, George! What about it?" challenged Uncle Ben, in full tilt again at the dragon.

Nora had pushed herself more securely into her chair. "I don't mind being laughed at, not a bit," she began. "Not myself. If I couldn't stand being laughed at, I'd go into a home for the feeble-minded. But I don't believe even you, Uncle Ben, would be talking quite so free if you'd been nearly drowned last night."

The strange dismal word resounded through the little lamplit room like the call of a bugle. Complete silence fell. Uncle Ben gaped where he stood. Then Mrs. Hopper crossed her legs viciously, and clasped her hands together.

"What kind of tale are you telling of us now?" she cried angrily.

Nora stared steadily into her mother's face. "I said drowned, Mother. I went out for a walk last night to "the Ponds". . . . It's nobody else's business—and I fell in."

"Fell in, my dear?" Mr. Hopper's voice rang dulcet as a bell in the midst of the baa-ings of a flock of sheep.

"Yes, Dad, and went clean under, too. Miles! It's deep there. But it was nothing to worry about. I soon scrambled out. But naturally," she drew her hand over her forehead, "it's given me a bit of a headache, perhaps."

"What I wouldn't wonder at, my fine lady,"

cried her mother, "is if you aren't in bed, come to-morrow morning, with a raging cold and inflammation of the lungs or something of that sort. Trapesing back all that way through the streets like a cod in a fishmonger's shop! *I* don't know what they'll think of you. And not to say a single word to your mother neither!"

"Feel my hand, Dad," said Nora. "That's cool enough, isn't it? There's nothing wrong with *me*, Mother. And I came back by the back-ways. It's when everybody begins talking, and I don't see why, and you all keep on at George—why, it makes *every*thing look silly. What *can't* be made to look silly? There's always those who'll laugh. But I'd rather not say anything more about it."

"Now, what I say," Uncle Ben as usual pranced gallantly to the rescue, "what I say is," he repeated, his two cold small eyes as grey-blue as agates on either side his long inquisitive nose, "is that's what they call a parable. Didn't I say an hour ago that George here had taken the plunge, and come up smiling? And what's Nora done else! *She* won't hurt. Bless you! Strong, healthy young creature like that, Polly. None of your lacksidasical young ladies that die of pneumonia from a draught not strong enough to blow the powder off their noses. She's all right. There now, Polly, she's all right. The prettiest of chips from the handsomest of blocks." He pushed himself in on to the little sofa beside his sister-in-law, and put his arm round her waist.

"Oh, you old fool!" retorted Mrs. Hopper with

amiable scorn, flinging his hand aside. "You are all fat, and nothing to fry! I've no patience with you."

But the position was saved, and Nora's only penalty was a good-sized couple of spoonfuls of Uncle Ben's whisky, in half a tumbler of scalding hot water.

"If you insist on gadding about by yourself in the dark, my girl, and having cold baths in public, you must take the consequences," said Mrs. Hopper, as she dropped two lumps of sugar into the steam.

Nora slipped out after George into the dusky passage.

"Honest, Nora," he breathed hoarsely into her ear, "you're not feeling *ill*?"

"Ill! Not me. I'll come along with you. George. Keep quiet. Stay *there*. I won't be a minute." She hastened up to her room. It was filled with a clear, still, darkening twilight. Her face glowed softly in the glass; and she could see dove-cote and greenhouse in the dark-shadowed garden below, as plainly as if they had been carved, by magic out of mystery, for the scene of a play. She paused in marvel of it a moment, then pulled on her hat and hurried softly out again. And George was waiting for her where she had left him. Like the Lion on the Brewery he hadn't moved the fraction of an inch.

"I like coming out when no one knows anything about it," she whispered, as he opened the door. "I'm tired of all that, George."

Not even the faintest of the fleeciest of clouds

showed in the sky above the double row of small brick houses in the empty street; and the air was crisp and cold—as if the small hours might bring a tang of frost. A waning moon was showing in the west, shedding her faint light into the crystalline, grey-blue sky.

The two of them walked on in silence until they reached the end of the street. A few hundred yards beyond the next, the branches of plane trees jutted out at right angles from their parti-coloured boles above the asphalt walks of the "Recreation Grounds". There was a faint musty odour in the air, mingled with that of autumnal flowers, beginning now to go to seed, in the borders around them.

"Honest, Nora, did you really *fall* into the Pond?" George asked. His voice still sounded slightly thick and inhuman, as if an animal were attempting to converse.

"You didn't think I was telling a lie, George?"

"I didn't think nothing about it, except you never told me. Do you often go out alone?"

Nora's breast rose beneath her jacket. "You *know* I often go out alone. And why shouldn't I? I like being alone. I shall always want to be alone when—when I want to be. There's no harm in that that I can see. I can take care of myself. Mother just talks. She wants things to go as *she* wants them to go."

"You might have been drowned in that Pond. It's a good eight feet deep near that upper bank. If that's what you call going out alone, why. . . ."

"But I didn't get drowned, or I wouldn't be here

now. As if catching cold and that stuff—why, what about them sillies that break the ice in the Serpentine all through the winter? And it wasn't the falling into the Pond that I was thinking about. It wasn't that at all."

"If you don't want to tell me nothing, I don't know as how I want to hear it," mumbled the young man in the billycock hat.

"Oh lor', George, for heaven's sake! There's a seat. Let's sit down."

The two of them seated themselves, a few inches coldly apart, in a dusk cast by a neighbouring lamp-post and by the increasing luminousness of the moon.

"When in the dark I went down into that Pond, George—and I *want* to tell you about it—it was not like what they say about such things. I seemed to be falling into an enormous black pit, and it seemed it would never end. But it wasn't, as they say, just *memories* that came back to me. There were horrible eyes staring at me, and voices shouting. No, not *at* me; but together, *across*. And when at last I came up again, and managed to breathe and to see a little, I was just clutching at anything and. . . . It was a lucky thing for me that stubby root was there."

But George had guessed, in some obscure groping fashion of his own, that this was not the end, was not even the important part of Nora's confession. He refused to be sympathetic. He sat stiff as a ramrod, staring straight in front of him under the brim of his hat. "You had no call to be there alone at that time of night. You had no call to be doing things secret-like."

Nora listened, her knees pressed tight together, her lips set hard. There would be time to argue when she had finished what she wished to say.

"But it wasn't just that that I'm trying to tell you. There isn't anything in that. It was what *happened. . . . Then.*"

George's mouth opened a little; his face groped round in her direction.

"It was the face I saw that won't . . . I keep on seeing it. I don't know how to explain. It was while, knowing I was safe, I was floating there in the water. It was there, above, looking at me; smiling at me, as if"—her speech had become more and more animated—"what I mean is, it wasn't a dream, it wasn't in my head, in my *mind*, as you might say. It wasn't *fancy*." The clear young voice trembled, as if in triumph at the word. "I *know* that. It was outside. *There*, a little above me, before my very eyes. I saw it, George, as I hung there in the water, and I wasn't excited, or scared, or struggling any more; I looked through my eyes, straight up at it. And by then I think the moon must have come out of the clouds. It was all silver on the water. And that face there—smiling at me. It seemed, as you might say, I had gone in under a dark dreadful tunnel, and come out the other side."

"Come out on what other side?" the young man blurted.

The Face

"Why, the other side"—Nora lifted her hand, as if she could make a picture of what she intended in the air. "The other side of all this, I mean. It was real. And yet it wasn't real. You might almost have been a child, it was so clear, so simple. And it's never left me. It's made everything different. You see, George, and oh, I *know* it sounds ridiculous—it was something to do with me myself." She stooped forward over her lap, staring hard at the asphalt beneath her foot. "And I don't know as how I've ever seen anything that. . . ." The square, young, ardent face turned sidelong a little—and lit with a vague, elusive smile he had never seen before—solemnly challenged the young man: "You aren't trying to help me much!"

George once more shifted uneasily in his seat.

"You told me to shut my mouth a minute ago. So I'm *keeping* it shut. You say you'd never seen him before?"

Nora burst out laughing. She listened to herself laughing—laughter as carefree as a green woodpecker's. "Seen *him* before! Oh, George! *Him!* I clean don't know what you're talking about! I never thought of it as being a him, and I didn't say it was, either. I've had enough of those claptrap islands of Uncle Ben's this evening, and all that widow talk, and I should have thought you had too. As if there wasn't anything but he's and she's to sniff and snigger about! As if there was nothing but silly jokes about just two people like you and me getting married, and all that. I don't know how they come to it, *that* I don't. What *I'm* saying is"—yet again the challenge rang out almost shrilly—"that's what I saw, and keep on seeing. And, I'm asking you, George, why shouldn't I? As if I cared what people think of me—as long as it's my own self. Who has any right, I should like to know, to say anything about what happens in anybody's *mind*?"

She looked away, paused, then turned almost tenderly to the young man.

"Oh, George, if only I could make *you* see it, too! I don't believe as you'd ever care to look at me again! There's pictures; but not like that. *I'm* nothing."

"And yet," cried the rational young man, "only a minute or two ago, on this very seat here, you were just making fools of us all for being he's and she's. As if that old Nosey! . . . I can't make out what you're getting at, and"—he gulped—"I don't know as how really I *want* to."

His voice died away. The earthy cold night air, having been rent asunder by its stridency, welled back unwounded, unreceptive. Not a soul was in sight, and that hastening footstep beyond the clustering trees might be nothing but a phantasm's for all that was actually visible.

Nora gazed vacantly. She was perfectly at ease, perfectly happy. All would come right. It was curious, indeed, when things looked so muddled and gloomy, that she should be conscious how strong and how free she felt in her body. It seemed that nothing she would ever attempt to do again could possibly fret or weary her—that she was capable of an infinitude of patience, of energy, and labour. But for the moment she must grope along gently and quietly.

"*This* is what I mean, George," she said, "if you will try and be a little patient. Did you ever see *any*-thing as if you had never *really* seen it before? I mean, more beautiful, as they say: more as though there was a sort of secret between you and it? Why, this lamp-light here now, George, on this old plank, on the wood; look at that! Do you see? There are two kinds of shadows of the leaves. They are like curious hands, webbed—like ducks' feet. And you can hardly tell where the dark and where the light begins. It's the moon and the lamp there; shining together: and here are you and me sitting here together too, and we don't know where it all comes from or what it all means, either. It's so *still*, George. I feel I could escape out of my body for ever and ever. Not that I want to: I'm too strong for that. But *that's* what I mean when I think about the face I'm telling you of. Only, much more. . . . It will all fade away and go, of course, but"—she turned eagerly—"supposing I'd sunk right down into that Pond again, under the willow trees, and my body had stayed there—well, I shouldn't be here now, talking to you, should I, George?"

"All I can say is", retorted the young man bitterly, "it's lucky your *mother* isn't hearing what you are saying."

The Face

"I'm leaving Mother out now," Nora said. "But I believe Father would understand a little what I mean. We don't *know*, George. You can't say that if I'd gone then, I'd be the same as I am now. I don't believe it. I don't believe that what I was *then*, sinking down as if for ever into that dark and cold and then looking up calm and peaceful at what was waiting there for me—is what I was when I was sitting there just now hearing Uncle Ben singing that silly rubbish, leering and going on like that, and all. He's soured—is Uncle Ben. And he doesn't want to show it."

"I don't see as how the songs were particularly silly, as you call it," George lied. "There's some like to take a high-and-mighty view."

"Well, never mind, George, they were," Nora said. "I didn't mean to be high and mighty; only just the truth. And it doesn't matter either way. If you want me, George, I suppose you've got to have all of me, but if you don't know what's there, you can't blame me if some of it's kept back. No, I don't mean that either. *No* one can ever have *all* of anybody, I mean. Now and then when I think of it, I'm almost sorry I didn't *not* come back last night. I'd *like* to be where that face came from. Why shouldn't I be, if it was my own? You can call it just a silly dream or you can call it a nightmare, if you like. What's words? It's what it meant to me that matters most, and if you can't put up with me, George, I don't know what we *shall* do."

The Face

Nora hadn't suspected that the nerves of the young man beside her were quite so near the snapping point. The only sound he uttered was a sort of breathless grunt as he stooped forward, his elbows on his knees, and hid his face in his hands, thrusting back his hard, round hat on his neatly oiled hair, as he did so.

"I don't know by what right——" Nora looked at him and looked again, "I don't know by what right you're taking what I've said like that, George. I needn't have told you at all."

"What I don't follow", replied a stubborn, almost blubbering voice, "is why anybody should want to hush up anything about their own faces. How could it have been more lovely-like if it *was* yours?"

"You didn't mean that so nice as it sounds! Haven't *you*—don't *you* carry about any picture of yourself better than the reflections of what you see in a glass? And even that's often better than real. You don't think, George, surely, it's just your *face* I love—and looking like that either! Why, it's you; *you*; what perhaps nobody else sees at all. We don't know where we come from, do we . . . ?"

"Keep your secrets," groaned the young man. "And I'll keep mine."

"If you call *that* secrets, George," she flamed, "then all I can say is, you're treating me mean. But, oh, you don't seem to see it. I've never been so happy as I was all the time when I was alone to-day sitting up there in my bedroom and you with your pigeons and the sunshine and all. And I thought—I thought perhaps you might understand. . . . I don't think I wish to be sitting here any more like this, now. We'll go home. . . ."

They walked in silence together till they reached the turn of the street, and then Nora slipped her firm hand into George's hard square one as he stalked along beside her. And so they arrived at No. 29. The lights had been put out in the sitting-room. Not a gleam showed between the Venetian blinds, but the moon had now begun to shine full on Allenbury Street. They came to a standstill. Nora drew her hand away, lifted her face, and looked up at the solitary glaring satellite.

"Won't you say a single word?" George breathed huskily. "You aren't going to leave me like that?"

Nora stooped forward, the hard brim of her young man's hat biting deep into her cheek as she did so.

"I don't believe as you're anything more than a child, George, when all's said. Are you jealous because my face is more lovely than *you'll* ever see it? *My* face! Lord!"

"You can't marry a child," George almost sobbed. "Promise. Nora, promise——"

Nora drew back. "I'll never promise a single thing," she retaliated. "As if you don't know that whatever was *not* me wouldn't just shed off like—like the skin from an onion. I'll just keep what I'll keep. And what I meant was, I'm glad to be back, but I'm gladder still to know . . ." She stared at the moon, squeezed the hard hand clutched in hers, but could get no further. And in less than a minute the door had closed behind her.

And George, a few tiny drops of dew chilling his face, having surveyed the glittering curtained windows, presently went on, along with his shadow, in his dark clothes and his round-topped hat, along the narrow, vast-skied, vacant, moon-glossed street.

THE CARTOUCHE

The clatter of the mowing-machine from beyond the laurel hedge had ceased. An almost complete silence had fallen—the silence of the ended. Every daisy that during the previous week had ventured to lift its eager face to the sun, every skulking or audacious dandelion had been swiftly beheaded. For lawns are lawns. They are intended to follow the even tenor of man's way, and not to indulge in the wild. The only sound that now interrupted the minute and steady click of Mrs. Millington's needle was the slightly rasping lament of a greenfinch, or the *whsst* of a swallow's wing, hawking low—stealthy as destiny—through the air of approaching evening.

Mrs. Millington's dark pretty head was stooping lower than appeared to be necessary over her sewing as she sat by the dark-framed wide-open window. The light cast up by the frilled linen pillow-case which she was mending paled the green reflected on cheek and brow from the sunlit leaves of the garden beyond and the intertwined bush of honeysuckle now languidly sweetening the sultry air.

The Cartouche

The sun would soon be setting—as it had set the evening before, and the evening before that. The sun of all her yesterdays indeed. But with how many different kinds of adieu!—cloudless, ardent, of fair promise; indifferent, cold, obscure. Soon would come twilight, then deepening dusk, then night. And at night, although her heart then became more restless with longing, with hope reiteratedly deferred and with an ever-encroaching despair, her mind and her thoughts were more closely her own.

Even now her eyes appeared to be intent on something a good deal further away than her needle. She had begun to think again; to feed upon memory. Then suddenly and not for the first time in these last few months, she had realized that thought itself *might* conceivably become audible. As if to make sure that this was not so, she glanced up stealthily into and across the room she was sharing—her husband's book-room.

Two quite different tastes, two natures and ages and upbringing were revealed in its furniture, its colours, its very ornaments. The senseless-looking clock of black marble on the mantelpiece—whose hands never failed to circle unflinchingly over its face to tell mutely what the exact "time" was in its own small share of normal human affairs—had been a gift to her husband from an old bachelor long-gone friend of his—a Dr. Edmund Briggs. No less clearly the worn-leather armchair in which he was now sitting, the lean knuckly fingers of his two large hands extending to the extremities of its two stuffed arms, had not been of her choosing. It was as masculine and durable as the benches in a railway waiting-room. The embroidered cushion which, on sitting down, he had carefully placed on the floor was feminine enough; not so the lamp-shade beside his chair, which was merely something to keep the light out of his eyes; nor the blotter on the leather-covered writing table, scattered untidily with books and papers. One hankers after one's own order of comfort in advancing age, and it becomes something of a virtue as well as a convenience to be domesticated. The foot-flattened-out green and red Turkey carpet was also as clearly an heirloom as was the portrait of Mrs. Millington's mother-in-law on the wall, whose painted eyes, it seemed, were now inhumanly surveying them both at the same time, and with some little asperity. It was a good likeness, but not a good picture; yet good enough for her son William, whatever his age—to recall her by, and perhaps so recall her candid counsel: when, that is, he paid any attention to it.

And now Mrs. Millington's exploring glance had settled on her husband again. Where had he been this last two days? And nights? Why was he so silent? Why did the expression on his brooding face suggest more than mere weariness? Sheer fag and even depression? And why wasn't he hungrily and audibly munching up his bread and butter? Was there—could there be—it had become a question recurrent as cockcrow—something wrong? Would the answer to it ever be in the affirmative? Once she had feared, and yet with a faint hope and relief, that it might be so. Now she feared this outcome no less, but with scarcely the faintest gleam of hope; with a sort of caged-in despair, rather. She pushed her silver thimble a little more firmly on to her finger, and began stitching again.

"Well, William?" she said. The lank, weary face, with its grey eyes and long nose, turned slowly a fraction of an inch in her direction.

"Yes, my dear?" he replied. "Oh? . . . I was only thinking!"

The non-committal smile that had died out over his face as he peered round at her might have been intended for a child; for, say, their small boy, Harold. But Harold, just now miles away at his prep. school, was fielding rather indolently at Long Stop.

"You are very silent. Even although you have only just come back? Can't you think and talk and munch and drink your tea at the same time? It isn't, you know, exactly the kind of absence which makes the heart grow fonder!" And as she listened to the vacuous words, it seemed as though she had memorized them ages and ages ago; as if they were the echo of a voice from another existence.

"I'm sorry, my dear: tiresome, tedious company, I'm afraid," he mumbled, through a half-suppressed yawn. "And yet—well, as a matter of fact, you'll never guess where I *have* been. I didn't know myself, so to say, until yesterday evening. I hope you weren't —weren't in the least anxious about me?"

She stitched on.

The Cartouche

"I *try*", she replied at length, "never to be anxious. About anything. I was a little surprised, of course; and wondered at your not coming home as you had arranged, and—at getting no message. But no; not—anxious. Why,"—and once more she seemed to be vacantly listening to something learned by rote "Why shouldn't you have a night off, now and again? I mean——" she stopped to bite off with her small teeth a cotton-end, which she now no less deliberately removed from the tip of her red tongue. "I mean, no one could say you weren't methodical, William."

"No? Oh, 'methodical', you mean. No." He bent forward, seized his cup, gazed at the grey-filmed brownish liquid in it, took a loud gulp, and sat back again.

"Well, I was a little afraid you might be. I was *dissuaded* from telephoning, you see. In a sort of way. And now that you have mentioned it, I can't really see why. Anyhow, there it is."

Mrs. Millington pondered on this a moment. "Perhaps", she replied, "your friend thought that if you did telephone, the wandering sheep would be dissuaded from *staying*? Lady or . . . ? Don't listen to me, William. I'm being nothing but a silly parrot. I *wasn't* anxious; I was only the least bit surprised—and extra glad to have you safely back. But now I'm terribly inquisitive. Unless of course it is, well, something private?"

"No," was the answer; "no marks for that, my dear. There's nothing private between you and me.

There never will be. Not from now. Nor was it a 'she' either. As a matter of fact, indeed, it was a 'he'. You look very charming in that light. I have always enjoyed seeing anybody sitting at an open window. I can remember, oh, years ago, my dear mother, and my poor Aunt Agnes too—she was always sitting at her open window during those last days. . . .

"Perhaps a storm is coming. It's strangely still this evening. Bless me, with that light on your face, you don't look a single day older than when—. On the contrary, this last year or so you have got positively younger, as if you had been sipping at the Fountain of Perpetual Youth. And I hope, my dear, you have, even although that, the change—I was reminded of it only last night again—would be nothing short of a calamity. The fact is, you should never have married me."

He had lifted his cup again, but refrained from drinking. The click of the needle had ceased. Without moving her head, Mrs. Millington had raised her dark eyes and was gazing out almost vacantly into the garden, as if she had forgotten or had taken no interest in what her husband had said. "Never married you?" she repeated. "But why not?"

"Because, you silly, magnanimous, heaven-sent creature, I am, in what matters most, perhaps, so stupid, habitual, matter-of-fact. *You* never were; and now, as tinder, I'm damper than ever."

She breathed again, almost with a sigh. "Oh, William. Again! I know all about that. That's a very old story. And who, pray, if it were true, is the 'silly'? Besides all that came back into your mind *after* you had been thinking. What about? and why? 'Last night'?" She could see only one greying cheek and a few tufts of her husband's grizzled hair, as he sat there lounging in his old shabby leather-covered arm-chair. He shifted his head round again to glance at her.

"Well, you see," he began methodically, "it was like this. You will only laugh at me. At Cambridge, when I got to the railway station, there was a train at a standstill *in* it. There was plenty of room. And the ticket collector told me that it was a fast one. And, for a wonder, so it proved to be. But the signal happened to be against us at one of the stations about half-way up. And it stopped. This woke me; I had been dozing. It was a lovely afternoon, very, very peaceful. I put my head out of the window and *there* was its name-board. Well, I thought to myself, this can't be chance. Indeed it seemed providential. I looked at my watch, realized that I should have at least two hours to spare at this end, seized my bag *and* hat *and* umbrella and got out. The train had begun to move—pretty fast—by then. Someone shouted, and the station-master all but threatened to report me. It appears that if trains, even if solely for their own convenience, stop at stations which they are not intended to stop at, no passenger is entitled to get out. It *suggests* pure Gilbert and Sullivan, but it's positively true and no doubt desirable. But imagine if life were like that! *Never* take advantage of an unexpected opportunity! *Never* follow an impulse!"

The Cartouche

There was an oddly hollow tone, a hint even of caution in the feminine comment that followed this not very original attack on railway by-laws. "But you may not be right. It's much more likely that it was because the train was already moving; and, as you said, pretty fast. That's dangerous at any—at any time; and I'm always warning Harold against it." She paused again. "What, William," she ventured at last, "was the name of the station? *What*, as you say, couldn't have been 'chance'?"

"Ah, there you are! You'd never guess. It was—Ebbingham! And of course I instantly thought of Louis. Had you realized, my dear, that we haven't seen or heard from him for *months*—why, not since June. Unless, perhaps, *you* did when I was in Warwickshire."

Mrs. Millington glanced up swiftly as if to make sure what her husband was looking at, at this moment. Her hand was trembling a little; and the colour had changed in her cheek. "Ebbingham!" she repeated. "You mean—you really mean, William, that you were foolish enough to take such a risk—like some headlong schoolboy. And so late in the day, without even knowing whether he was at home. No wonder I was a little anxious. And then, about trains. You *say* you hadn't heard. But surely you remember I told you that his sister—I dislike her so much that I can't even recall her name for the moment—Oh, yes, Mildred—that I told you we had met by chance in town, and that she had said he was going away? I am sure I told you."

"Alas, my dear," said her husband, still staring at the fan-shaped piece of paper concealing his empty grate, "I don't remember. But no doubt you are right. You are too kind to this rapidly decaying memory of mine. It's getting worse and worse; I was reminded of it too only yesterday. Anyhow, there it is. I had been wanting to have a word with him about the examinations next month and he is very dilatory; but it would have involved a long letter; and I am tired—just a little. So why not? Nothing venture, nothing win. Anyhow, I was out of the train and in the only cab available before I had realized he might not be at home."

"Yes? . . . Was he?"

"Oh, rather. We had quite a business talk. A good talk, too—within limits. He showed little surprise and no dismay at seeing me; or anyhow, it wasn't noticeable. Rather the contrary even; he *might* almost have been expecting me. He seemed very well too; a bit absent perhaps. But then, he always appears to have two minds at work at the same time. Did you ever know a more zigzag talker?

"I forgot all about the trains; tea came in, we talked on and on, long after we had finished our little business matters; and then he said something about taking pot luck; and—well, would I make a night of it? There was no way out of that—unless I preferred to face getting home in the small hours. Unfortunately, as I say, his telephone was out of order. And I couldn't very well suggest that you might be anxious. He's changed. Had you noticed that? Of course, one never could predict what he might not do next. He *seems* happy-go-lucky enough; and yet never somehow quite at his ease. A queer blend. I should think in fact he had positively practised most 'nexts'. All impulse one minute and the wisdom of the serpent the next. He interests me. He's thinner; but not a bit less—well, attractive, I suppose. But *you* would know best about that. I find it so difficult in some things to get the woman's point of view. There's a kind of challenging Faust-like adventurousness in his face. And I'm not perfectly sure if one can positively and finally depend upon him. One can't always be certain what he is after. I supposed for a while that he had invited me to stay on because he wanted to consult *me* about something. But that must have been a mistake. . . . And—but there, my dear, what a disastrous thing it would be if the power were suddenly conferred on us to share one another's thoughts—without any words, I mean."

Mrs. Millington had sat, her hands in her lap, motionlessly listening, her eyes still fixed on the darkening scene beyond the window, as if she were waiting for something to happen; or was in search of something within her mind, but mislaid.

"I had no notion, William," she said at length, "that you dissected your—that you analysed people like that. To such an extreme. And why 'disastrous'? I can't quite see, either—if he *had* nothing to consult you about—why you should have fancied

otherwise. As for sharing people's thoughts. . . ."
Her voice had fallen a little flat and she failed to
finish the sentence.

Her husband glanced back at her again, over his
glasses. "Why, yes, though you may not know it, I
share your thoughts sometimes," he assured her—
almost with the shyness of a child confiding a secret.
"But it's Louis I was thinking of. I can't really make
him out. 'Dissect', indeed! He's so unpredictable,
elusive, keeps to cover—in spite of all that gaiety,
all that charm. I don't mean to suggest any definite
antipathy. The truth is my old wits are a bit too
sluggish for him; always have been. Anyhow, it
wasn't really *that* I had in mind. As I say, we had a
long talk; I'm not a bad listener, and I thoroughly
enjoyed it. But for that very reason perhaps I drank
too much of his special whisky, so it began to
languish a little towards midnight. None the less
there was again that feeling of something definite
coming and yet failing to come. As when one wants
to sneeze, and can't. Actually, it was involved in the
dream I was going to tell you about. In the best
guest-chamber too; and I pay my respects to Louis's
or his housekeeper's taste in curtains and bed linen.
Unless he has other help."

"In the guest-room? *There*, you mean? Last
night?"

"Yes, indeed; in the guest-room; a very pleasant
room, too. You don't know the house, of course—I
mean its upper parts?"

She fixedly returned his absent stare.

"We have only been there two or three times, William—to luncheon."

"So it was: twice," replied her husband, after another gulp at his cold tea and even a bite of his thin bread and butter. "And one doesn't have luncheon in the guest-room, darling, does one?"

But to this little sally, and one so absurdly inviting an easy witticism, Mrs. Millington said nothing. Her sewing lay in her lap, both her hands were pressed down into it as if it didn't matter in the least how much tumbled and creased the delicate fabric became.

"The real point," continued her husband, "is not so much the dream, but something that followed it; a sort of confession, my dear. Have you time, the patience to listen for—well, perhaps another ten whole minutes?"

There was nothing to show that she had heard the question, except that she replied in a low, ridiculously serious voice, "Of course I can listen, if only —well—you'll go straight on. Why couldn't we have *begun* at the dream? Anyone would suppose . . ."

She broke off, rose from her chair, and sat down again. "The clouds are gathering—look! Up and up and up. There's going to be a storm. I have a headache. But here I am; I want to hear the dream—and the rest. On the other hand, William, if the thunder begins . . . well, you see, I couldn't."

Certainly the sun had left the garden, and the gloom that now lay over it in a dead and menacing quietude and stagnation was not that of an ordinary twilight. Still, presages of storm often cheat even the weather-wise in a climate so fickle as England's; and everything might blow over.

"Well," her husband was continuing meditatively, "it was a very odd dream, odd to me at any rate; but other people's dreams are so dreadfully wearisome and always seem so pointless. I wish, indeed, my dear, you hadn't a headache." His voice had become a little plaintive. "I, too, have just the rudiments of one. The same cause, thunder perhaps; but more likely Louis's whisky. Well, as I say, we talked until nearly midnight. He told me how one can avoid the effects of taking too much! His tongue darts about like a dragon-fly, never staying for more than a moment on any single subject or object. Nor does his eye. I found it wearisome at last. Besides, whether right or wrong, I had the impression that much of it was talking for talking's sake, that he must be in some anxiety, had perhaps something on his mind, wished perhaps that I hadn't come; though there was nothing, except, perhaps, his manner, to suggest it, and—his occasional silences. He *is* an oddity, you know, Margaret: so mercurial, and unstable perhaps. I wonder what you yourself really think of him? Is what I say anything like your view of him too?"

Mrs. Millington was re-threading her needle, and with an obstinate cotton-end, and in the failing light. "Yes," she said at last; "I should imagine it *is* much the same. Aren't all—temperamental people like that? restless and impulsive? You mean, I suppose, that he is unlikely to stay fixed in any one intention, is never sure of his own mind? Is that what you mean?" But the faint voice that had put the question seemed not to be in any need of an answer. It was as if, in spite of the tense silence, she would not even be interested in any reply.

"What baffles me most of all", said her husband, "is that he has never yet been able to fix his *heart* on anything. The truth is, my dear, he ought to have found a wife somehow—long ago. Perfectly easy! Not that my congratulations to her would not have been tempered with misgivings."

"What *was* the dream, William?"

"Well, as I say, I got to bed very late. A charming room, too, facing south: otherwise the moonlight couldn't have got in through the curtains. Louis has 'taste' enough to run an 'antique' furnishing shop. And yet he lets his roof leak."

"His roof leak?"

"I'll come to that later. As you know, I am very rarely favoured with a dream and when I am, I usually fail to remember it. Nor are hieroglyphics" —he laughed softly to himself—"my strong point. Anyhow, when I awoke, it was, I suppose, about two o'clock in the morning. Suddenly and softly wide-awake—as though I had been called, as though a drowsy voice had called me. I had dreamt that I was lying face upwards on a very low bed, immured in the deep, dark, stony bowels of a pyramid, but without the least knowledge of how I had managed to get there, and convinced that there was no way out—not even by the way by which I must have come in.

"I was terrified, and in acute distress. In the faint, dusky light, I could see that there was a very fine sand on the floor, and a few old broken or derelict relics of objects which I couldn't distinguish—sacred furniture and images, I suppose. The place appeared to have been rifled; but there was no trace, as far as I can recall, of any sarcophagus or of any mummy, although some sort of both presumably there must once have been. Was *I* the mummy?

"The sand was of the finest dust on the stony floor, and the walls were arabesqued with inscriptions— flowers, figures, serpents and so forth. I was only vaguely aware of this, for my attention had become fixed on one small oblong lozenge-shaped hiero-glyphic or cartouche.

"As you know, a cartouche usually contains the characters of some sovereign's name; Cleopatra's has two birds in it—heads to the west—as indeeed hers finally was! Apart from this there was no other design that I can recall on the stone ceiling over my head. Where the light was coming from I cannot say; in sleep perhaps our own eyes supply it, like a cat's. The characters in the cartouche resembled, left to right, first a crouching animal with a child's face; tiny, I surmise, of course, but greatly dream-magnified. It was also very lovely. Next, there was a tree—a willow or weeping ash, something of that kind; and next to that, and partly under it, stood what appeared to be a box or chest or tomb with a rounded top—of the shape of a sarcophagus but much smaller. There was even a sort of sullen glitter from the precious stones with which it had been inlaid—although, as I say, this was only a representation of it. I realized that it had once contained the vital parts of some inmate, the heart, viscera and so forth; but that now it was empty. The astonishing thing is that I knew in my dream perfectly well what all these emblems stood for and what they signified. A desperate cankering grief for one thing—the *weeping* willow. An inward descent towards death. It was as if the past had resolved itself into this tiny esoteric pattern and that I could grasp it in an instant of time, and interpret its every single syllable as briefly. 'The secrets of all hearts,' my dear. But *that* was in the dream."

Mrs. Millington had been so intent on this fantastic and muddled narrative that she had hardly stirred since her husband had begun to relate it. But although a dream, so comparatively commonplace, could hardly be the cause of her repressed excitement, it was almost as if in entreaty or reproach that she put her next question: "William, you aren't making all this up? You aren't playing with me? It *was* a dream?"

"I am telling you everything precisely as I recall it," was his reply. "But listen; you must await the sequel. That is what is going to be my real little difficulty. And I shall feel all the better when it is over. All that was just the dream. What, when I *woke*, I knew, or at any rate supposed, to be the meaning of the emblems, of the complete design of the cartouche—and please don't scoff—was just this and only this. It meant, 'It was Here'. 'It happened Here'. Although I hadn't the faintest conception *what*! It sounds ludicrous, but that was absolutely all. But although as is the way with dreams, I took it to be a sort of personal and private message or communication, it must merely have referred of course to the unhappy fate, the destiny—who knows what?—of the poor creature, the mummy that had been interred there, in its stony sepulchre. At least so one may *surmise*. Well, so much for the dream."

The ageing face, again turned sidelong and away from her, looked fagged and colourless and depressed, as if it were still in some degree enslaved by a mere illusion; and the eyes in it were once more fixed upon the ceiling overhead, although this appeared to be completely unintentional and innocent of any design. Once more untidy tufts of grizzled hair were showing grotesquely above the darkened leather of the chair and the awkward contents of it resembling an old-fashioned tailor's dummy partially dismembered. Not that the owner of them would have been concerned in the least at what he looked like; he preferred "taking things as they come" and had never been in the habit of paying much attention to appearances: although his memory sometimes managed this unaided.

"The fact is," he went on, "I can't bear mysteries. Things in this world should be plain and above-board; as far, at any rate, as we humans can make them. And why a silly foolish inconsequent dream like that should leave any more impression than a child's picture book on the waking rational mind I cannot conceive—if, that is, one's mind *is* ever completely rational. No doubt these psycho-analysts could make hay, and pretty sour hay at that, of the whole thing. Whether or not, and I don't care, it has haunted me ever since. You see, *then* I knew the meaning of it; and to know all, they say, is to forgive all. But now it's gone.

"Besides, somehow or other, this seemed to be not merely and only a dream. For without being conscious of any transition from sleeping to waking, I presently, as I say, found myself lying on my back in Louis's ornate and luxurious but most comfortable four-poster—staring up at *his* virgin plaster. The merest trickle of moonlight was edging in between the grey-blue window-curtains, causing the sort of dusky gloom that had seemed to be the illumination of my stony cell in the pyramid; yet it cast a pale narrow shaft of light clean across the ceiling. If she had not been well past the full this couldn't of course have happened; though I don't profess to be much of a moon expert. In fact, my dear, I claim to fall just that much short of being the "compleat" lunatic. There was light enough at any rate to show up vaguely the actual pattern of the stain on the whitewash—the stain, I mean, made by the rain that had leaked through the roof, or through the floor-boards perhaps of an attic above me, owing to

The Cartouche

Louis's loose tiles. To *that* degree we are both of us lunatics!

"However that may be, there, sure enough, was the general design of the cartouche. And no doubt merely because the dreaming mind or fancy is so densely thronged with symbols which are supposed to be hints or warnings to the waking consciousness, I detected in the patterns precisely the same details as those of the dreamed-of hieroglyphics. Not only that; for some minutes together I accepted the same ridiculous interpretation: 'It was Here'. *It happened Here.* And naturally, I was pestered by exactly the same question—What?

"Well, all old beds—and Louis's also—unless, which is quite possible, it is a fake, is Elizabethan—all old beds must not only have had scores of nocturnal occupants, but must have witnessed many uneasy, wakeful, miserable and possibly even tragic nights. Peaceful, pleasant, amorous, happy and visionary ones too. One is born, one marries, one dies; and all three usually involve a bed of some kind—from W.S.'s 'second-best' to Procrustes'. They say, you know, that what are called ghosts may be merely an outcome, impressing the imagination of the living, of tragic events that have left their indelible mark on the inanimate objects around them. Why not a bed, then? Why not?"

He had paused again, but not as if in wait for any critical comment or appreciation, since he had at once hastened on with: "I don't *want*, my dear, naturally enough, to destroy my own little romance.

But truth must out. When the very neat parlour-maid came in with my tea and drew back the grey-blue curtains, I had a good long look at Louis's rain-stain in the full unflattering light of morning. Natur-ally. And, believe it or not, there was scarcely a vestige of the pattern I had seen in it in the small hours. It was now no more than a lozenge-shaped blur which you could, if you wished, turn either into a catafalque with mourning plumes complete, or into some bower of delight out of the *Faerie Queen* —whichever most suited your fancy."

For some minutes Mrs. Millington had been sit-ting, her chin cupped in her hands, her elbows on her knees, her eyes fixed on the open window, as if she were positively gloating on the intense stillness of the garden and its celestial canopy—like some moulting bird too far gone to chirp or stir, and peering out of the bars of its familiar cage at the vision of unattainable freedom beyond them, or even at a freedom now become impracticable, tarn-ished and stale. The slightly sallow cheek no longer owed any artificial green to the reflected sunlight; the dark eyes resembled motionless pools in some mountain valley on a starless night, wherein the reflections of the preceding centuries have left nothing but opacity and eclipse.

"I haven't", she said at length, "been really able to follow a good deal of that last part, William— about the ceiling and the rain-stains and the moon. After you woke up, I mean. Do you mean that what you saw in the dream was caused by a sort of distortion of the actual pattern in the ceiling? In that case surely you must have seen it—perhaps in the few moments before you fell asleep. And yet you say that, after all, the pattern wasn't really like that at all. It was merely a blur. Besides, no mere rain-stain, surely, could resemble so closely a child, a tree *and* a tomb? Can't it have been mere fancy, William, do you think—such as one so often, and without any such intention, re-creates in one's memory?"

"I am sorry, my dear, for telling it all so badly. But I do mean that the rain-stain by *moon*light resembled that. My explanation, right or wrong, is pretty much what you have suggested—that I must have seen, without definitely observing, the stain on the ceiling before going to sleep; that this caused the dream; and that it was the dream that imposed the design or pattern—at least to some extent—upon it. It was merely a mixture of states of mind, the dreaming and the half-dreaming and the awakening. When, then, as I say, Louis's elegant parlourmaid tapped at my door with my tea, and——"

As if the word itself had actually summoned her, Mrs. Millington's own parlourmaid at this moment herself opened the door and came in to take the tea-things away. Mr. Millington watched her until the door was shut again.

"What a marvellous crop of hair that girl has," he remarked. "You don't often see red hair nowadays: or not, at any rate, that sort of golden bronze tint. Mark my words, you won't keep *her* for very long. . . . I wish none the less she wouldn't interrupt.

But there, my dear, I mustn't bore you any longer—not for more than one more minute, anyhow; as it is for that I have been waiting. As I was saying, the moment I awoke, I turned my head to look for my dream-cartouche, and the actual disfiguring rain-stain in the morning light no more resembled it than the face I am now turning towards you resembles what it was like, say, about thirty years ago, when you were a little girl with pigtails and aged ten. In those days I was not such a very bad-looking young man, though you might not think it now. And there's the rub."

The vigilant and constricted expression that had steadily deepened on Mrs. Millington's face during this long and wearisome recital, after lifting a little, had intensified again.

"Oh, William," she broke out, "if only you wouldn't keep straying off in what you have to tell me. What '*rub*'? I don't know what you mean. I'm dreadfully tired, dreadfully stupid, nervy, worked up. It's this heaviness in the air. Though now, it seems, the storm is not going to break after all. It's less dark. I dread thunder—am a coward in any crisis. And yet I wish—I wish almost anything. If only it would clear! Oh, everything!—the air! To breathe again! One's very soul. How you can have managed to keep all this out of your talk at lunch just passes my comprehension. You merely said the trains had gone wrong. Not a word about any dream. Nothing. And even now you haven't finished. *What* 'rub'?"

146

The Cartouche

"For one reason, you precious, silly, troubled, patient thing, it was because everything I have been telling you concerns solely you and me. I sat as mum as a Grampus at breakfast that next morning, except to congratulate Louis on making his guests so comfortable—and an unexpected guest at that. I don't imagine that *he* would be very patient with dreams. Not at least with other people's. Not even with his own, perhaps—, for very long together. He's so restless, so self-centred, so precarious. I came to the conclusion, my dear, the moment I was in my cab again, that he and I don't match. I'm sluggish oil; *he's* water and—unstable. Let's drop him out; and the dream too into the bargain. I believe even, as a matter of fact, that deep in your own heart, you share my prejudice.

"However, the 'rub' is this. Somehow that silly and meaningless cartouche took me back to when I was about twenty. It was in part a memory, you see; and it was concerned in part with a tree very much like my dream-tree, but not with anything in the nature of a chest or tomb—except perhaps in its general shape. My actual memory of those far-away days is of a tree; late dusk; autumn; a plain damp backless wooden bench. And two anguished people sitting on it."

He rose from his chair, yawned, shuddered, and drawing up another next to his wife's, sat down beside her and laid both his long bony hands over hers and her sewing.

"I want you", he said, "to listen very carefully to

what I am going to tell you, and then to declare quite frankly if it will make the least difference to us. It cannot but alter your ideas of me, what you think of me, what you believed of me. But it's all far away, remote, boxed up in the past; it *was*—well, until yesterday—all but forgotten—put out of mind, I mean. There never yet was any real opportunity of its being forgiven; and it's not for me—not for myself—to forgive it now."

His wife had managed to withdraw her left hand from beneath his own, the other remained a prisoner. She was breathing so rapidly that she could hardly articulate clearly.

"I haven't the least notion", she said, "what you are going to tell me. Whatever it is, it could not make any difference now. It is, you say, far away; and you were young; and, and human—like the rest of us, young *and* old. What *are* we, when all is said? Like bits of elastic, that can stretch so far, but no farther. Then we snap. Nor could it make any difference to what some day, *some* day . . . Oh, William, please let me go now. My head is racking; I can hardly see out of my eyes. All you can mean is that this tree of your dream, of your waking and of the past, and those two woeful young people on the wooden seat—why, both, as such, must have rotted away by this time—all you can mean is that men, women, all of us, just because we are human, cannot for ever be fixed in anything, cannot remain absolutely steadfast and unchanged. The failure, the broken hopes, the futile yet lovely romanticalness

are in our very natures; and we have, if we are foolish and impetuous, and give away the heart without
counting the cost—we have to pay the price, whatever that may be or mean. You were going to tell
me about some old love affair, weren't you? I can see
her—sweeter, simpler, more impulsive, better-
natured far, far than I have ever been, could be; and
I suppose, circumstances, something you weren't
responsible for, something perhaps you *were* responsible for—well, came in between. Perhaps you even
treated her with atrocious unkindness? Well, what
then? What we want, what we desire, changes,
fades out, William. We cannot help ourselves—not
even when we have attained it. Most of us. But the
heart itself doesn't change; only its wants. And if it's
that, I don't wish, I don't want you to tell me any
more. I can see by your face—your hands are cold—
that I have guessed right."

She suddenly fell silent, staring at him in the
faintly lightening gloom of the open window. "It's
strange, isn't it? Very strange? If that hadn't happened, if you two had never parted, we ourselves
would never have met? We should never even have
met."

THE PICTURE

Lucia drew back overtly at last from the shelter and shadow of the crimson black-lined curtain. Its folds screened an upper window—a shallow bow in shape. From out of its small panes she had been watching her husband. In this last strange year, the first of her married life, she had learned many things about him. She had learned that his loyalty and tenderness, his unwearying secret consideration for her, were not merely due to the funny little fact that simply could not be denied—that he was years and years older than she was; but also because he was wholly himself and—well, loved her. As she loved him? That question, as she had stood, one hand gently resting on the curtain, her dark eyes fixed, had again crept like some predatory little animal into her thoughts. Could it possibly be as much? . . . This dreadful question of age. He seemed to be so much less apprehensive of his leaving her than was she of his going. Besides . . .

The rounded lids above her unusually dark eyes echoed, as it were, the curve of cheek and chin. Her other hand lay on her breast. The sun shone hot on the flawed eighteenth-century glass of the white-framed window. This room of her husband's was like a little hothouse in the sunshine of early afternoon; and presently she would draw the black-lined crimson curtains again to keep it cool for his coming back.

Another thing she had learned was, that, to him, habit of spirit, mind and body resembled the serene sky of a St. Martin's Summer. Then why—instead of quietly busying himself with trowel or spud—was he merely standing looking down on a bed crammed with Sweet Williams in full bloom? Palest pink, auricular-eye, scarlet, blood-red, deepest crimson—his favourite flower.

"Second childhood, my dear," he had remarked more than once, as they had stood there admiring them together. "I might as well be five again, in a holland pinafore, and my mother. . . . Hundreds of years ago."

Oh yes, that was all very well, but it could not surely, explain his present dejected attitude? Or similar far-away ponderings, meditations, usually ending when challenged with an unintended sigh and a prolonged smile—a smile somehow not the less inscrutable because it was so loving. Why should loving anybody ever leave *any* human heart sorrowful? Whereas—pent-up, hot, and reviling herself beyond words, realizing, her own miserable jealousy—it now often left her not only sorrowful but almost faint with doubt and remorse?

With one sweep of her arm she drew the curtain

across the window, and turned, completely concealed by it, towards the portrait again. She knew by
rote every inch of it. She was letter-perfect. Harriet,
his first love, his first wife. A second string of course
need not play the less sweetly because there was once
a first. It is itself to blame if it jar its own music. She
had married, realizing perfectly well that in every
human soul there is room for two, for three or four,
perhaps, and that no beloved image in a heart of any
depth and fidelity can ever wholly oust, or be
ousted, by another.

She knew too that for weeks past she had con-
sistently ignored what had rapidly become a sort of
idiotic and even frightening obsession. Age cannot
but live a good deal in the past, and especially perhaps
in the company of a long-gone childhood. She didn't
mind, in the least, complete hours stolen from her in
tender remembrances of that kind; so far-away and
enduring too. But couldn't he, *shouldn't* he have seen
that this portrait—with its never-ceasing share of a
life beyond the grave—was all wrong. And for all
three of them?

It was mean, odious, idiotic, and yes—why deny
it—an almost insane speculation, to let anything like
that fester and corrupt in her mind. And yet in her
present nerve-racked unfamiliar condition she could
no more rid herself of this mental misery than one
can immediately cure any bodily ill. She had tried—
bitterly, intensely—and had failed. Day by day to
continue to enter this room, whether vacant or with
her husband there, quietly reading or writing in his

chair, and that smiling painted phantom on the wall
continually surveying the scene which she had been
compelled to abandon had become an impossible
burden. Merely to discover somehow, without any
direct question—impossible thought!—without any
sinuous probings even, exactly how she stood, and
how *she* stood! This at last had seemed to have become a sheer necessity. She couldn't bear the sus-
pense. If—in her present condition it could not be
satisfied—well, how live on? Like this?

Once a busy spectre begins to frequent the mind,
you never—she had discovered this long ago—you
never know even yourself what devils it may not at
length invite in.

Her husband's thinning face, those tranquil grey-
blue eyes, that had yet recently shown so many
marks of weariness, what were they concealing?
What *could* they be concealing—except thoughts,
remembrances, and perhaps even gnawing regrets
which she could not possibly share? How was it
possible to bring him to realize what was corroding
away in her every vestige of her peace of mind? It
was as if she had discovered a viper curled up in her
work-basket. The answer to that question had stolen
upon her only a day or two before.

Awakened suddenly and silently in the small
hours as if a cold lean hand had gently shaken her by
the shoulder, the vile device seemed to have sprung
up in her sleeping mind like Jonah's gourd. This bold
and too-large portrait had scarcely ever been even so
much as referred to between them. Why should it

have been? It portrayed, not the Harriet who six years ago had died and left him, but the Harriet of at least twenty years before that. Very fair, yet not beautiful, at least not beautiful to most unheeding eyes. A young face, and yet a face full of the past, a face out of some old extravagant romantic story, a face unaware of what just one glimpse of it might bestow, a face which if it were once beloved—no matter what might happen—could be ever really unbeloved: not deep within; and never forgotten. Forgotten! Why at this moment, as if in the mere fact that it was refusing to look at her, it was an irresistible, an unendurable reminder of her own miserable trick.

Hating herself, as might a reptile engaged in devouring its own tail, she had stolen down from her bedroom in the small hours and had lit one of the candles here, on her husband's writing table. Not even the angel Gabriel could have persuaded him to burn electric light. Perhaps she had been not quite awake. And certainly a nightmare mind can manage things the day mind would retch at. However that might be, with an infinite disgust, she had at last mounted a chair and, with the utmost caution and skill, first by igniting, then by extinguishing the tiny flame, burned through about two-thirds of the thickness of the cord behind the picture by which it was suspended from the wall. Even the rotation of the earth may affect at last a hanging picture. So may a mere draught, the jar of traffic, passing footsteps and the slow secret incessant tug of the force of gravitation. Its fate might then prove suspended by a thread. Its downfall could be only a question of days. And then, surely, surely, he would be bound to betray himself. She would at last *know*.

It was perhaps in part her passionate nature that had made her so superstitious. Was *he*? Strangest of facts, she couldn't really tell. Not for certain. With a faintly whimsical smile, he would do a dare and walk in bravado under a ladder—paint-pot or no paint-pot. He *preferred* other numbers to 13. At sight of a magpie and solely on his own account he would turn his head, spit, laugh and apologize. Once when she herself, after he had stolen behind her and put his hand over her eyes, had struggled free and had seen, through glass, the exquisite gold thread of the crescent moon tilted very low (the old moon in the new moon's arms)—when his very aim had been to prevent this—he had seemed really shaken.

He had seized her hands, had kissed her cheek and mouth almost frenziedly, saying, "There, it must be all right now, mustn't it? God forbid!"

Well, surely if he was as superstitious even as that, she couldn't but surprise some exclamation, some instinctive disclosure, some dreadful change of face when in its own moment the portrait should crash to the ground! And now, she herself never for an instant ceased to be awaiting that crash. If she had not come to hate and detest the face it portrayed perhaps?—but it was too late now. Or *was* it too late?

She stole soundlessly to the window again. An age

seemed to have passed since she had last looked out. It could have been only a few moments. Her husband was where she had left him. Soon, he would begin his afternoon's potterings. There was Turner, watering-can in hand, coming towards him. How dreadfully weary, narrowed in, even disconsolate he looked, as if all but worn out by some inward struggle. A shuddering revulsion of feeling came over her. Think of it! Some day she might perhaps be looking back on this from beyond an awful gulf of utter darkness. An evil done, even if it remain undiscovered, is an ineradicable horror, a scar no power in earth or heaven could ever remove.

Well, she was awake *now*. She must do her utmost to undo what she had done, and must chance discovery. Trembling knees and hands, she dragged up a chair, mounted it, and with both arms extended attempted to lift the portrait from the wall. To snap and re-knot the string while it hung there was out of the question. But the frame was heavier even than she had expected. The cord refused to unloop itself from its hook. Her heart continued steadily thundering against the cage of her ribs. She tried again, and was compelled to desist. Very gradually she allowed the portrait to slide down the full length of the cord again; but the strain was too great, and even as, with a murderous splintering of glass, it crashed to the floor she heard his step along the corridor outside. In sheer panic she leapt from the chair, stumbled, all but fell, attempted to escape and met him full in the doorway.

"Why, my dear, my dear! You poor thing, what's wrong? What's the matter?"

Her teeth were chattering, she had begun to hiccough.

"I tried, I tried," she was almost shouting at him. "I had been watching you. I was anxious about you. Don't look. Come away. It was a miserable deception—worse. I can't bear it."

" 'Watching me'?" he repeated. " 'Couldn't bear it'—can't bear what?" His face had gone a deadly grey, even his lips. "Just *that*? My own dear, loved, loving thing. How can *that* matter? . . . 'Anxious about me'? I should have to have told you soon. But I don't understand. Why, only a week or two ago I—you know how mere time wears out everybody, and I. . . . And now", he added turning towards the wall, "*this* horrible thing has happened. It must have startled you to death."

Still clasping her hand, he stooped over the portrait lying face downwards on the floor, and lifted the end of the severed cord. No attentive eye could have been deceived by that.

"Why!" he began meditatingly. "How queer! That's not an ordinary. . . . It's charred. It's been. . . ."

Releasing her hand, he turned to look at her. The dark distraught face, fingers clenched, eyes shut, seemed to be as brightly illuminated in the half-curtained room as some ridiculous painted clown's in the limelight of the stage.

"It was I, me," she was saying. "I fancied she—you—I. I *must* go now. What did you mean, what did you *mean* by 'I should have told you soon'? Not that—*that*." She nodded her head towards the fallen portrait.

"That!" he exclaimed. "You poor precious angel thing. My dear, my dear! *That!* Why, I hadn't a notion! It was only—only the letter that came from —that was enclosed with Dr. Brown's. I fancied you had guessed it had—it had not been very favourable. But my own dear; we had both foreseen it, known it, realized it—underneath? Hadn't we? When one is so old . . . well, one can't go on— indefinitely." The words ceased. He was gazing at the back of the picture. . . . "What a lucky thing", he added, smiling up into her face, "that we knew all along things weren't quite right."

THE QUINCUNX

On opening the door and in no good humour at so late and apparently timid a summons I fancied at first glance that the figure standing at the foot of the four garden steps was my old and precious friend Henry Beverley—unexpectedly back in England again. At the moment there was only obscured moonlight to see him by and he stood rather hummocked up and partly in shadow. If it hadn't been Henry one might have supposed *this* visitor was the least bit apprehensive.

"Bless my heart!" I began—delight mingled with astonishment—then paused. For at that moment a thin straight shaft of moonlight had penetrated between the chimney stacks and shone clear into the face of a far less welcome visitor—Henry's brother, Walter.

I knew he was living rather dangerously near, but had kept this knowledge to myself. And now in his miniature car, which even by moonlight I noticed would have been none the worse off for a dusting, he had not only routed me out, but was also almost supplicating me to spend the night with him—in a house which had, I heard with surprise, been left to him by an eccentric aunt, recently deceased—about two miles away.

Seldom can moonshine have flattered a more haggard face. Had he no sedatives? Sedatives or not, how could I refuse him? Besides, he was Henry's brother. So having slowly climbed the stairs again, with a lingering glance of regret at the book I had been reading, I extinguished my green glass-shaded lamp (the reflex effects of which may have given poor Walter an additional pallor) pushed myself into a great-coat, and jammed a hat on my head, and in a moment or so we were on our way, with a din resembling that of a van-load of empty biscuit-tins. I am something of a snob about cars, though I prefer them borrowed. It was monstrous to be shattering the silence of night with so fiendish a noise, all the blinds down and every house asleep. "On such a night . . ." And as for poor Walter's gear-changing —heaven help the hardiest of Army lorries!

"Of course," he repeated, "it would be as easy as chalk to dismiss the whole affair as pure fancy. But that being so, how could it possibly have stood up to repeated rational experiment? Don't think I really care a hoot concerning the 'ghostly' side of this business. Not in the least. I am out for the definite, I am dog-tired, and I am all but beaten."

Beaten, I thought to myself not without some little satisfaction. But beaten by what, by whom?

"Beaten?" I shouted through the din. We were turning a corner.

"You see—for very good reasons I don't doubt—
my late old aunt could not away with me. She found
precious little indeed to please her in my complete
side of the family—not even the saintly Henry. My
own idea is that all along she had been in love with
my father. And I, thank heaven, don't take after *him*.
There is a limit to imbecile unpracticality, and—" he
dragged at his hand-brake, having failed to notice
earlier a cross-road immediately in front of us under
a lamp-post.

"She never intended me to inherit so much as a
copper bed-warmer, or the leg of a chair. Irony was
not her strong point—otherwise I think she might
have bequeathed me her wheezy old harmonium. I
always had Salvation Army leanings. But Fate was
too quick for her, and the *house* came to *me*—to me,
the least beloved of us all. At first merely out of
curiosity, I decided to live in the place, but there's
living and living, and there's deucedly little cash."

"But she must have . . ." I began.

"Of course she must have," he broke in. "Even
an old misbegotten aunt-by-marriage can't have
lived on air. She *had* money; it was meant, I believe
—she mistrusted lawyers—for my cousin Arthur and
the rest. And"—he accelerated—"I am as certain as
instinct and common sense can make me, that there
are stocks, shares, documents, all sorts of riff-raff, and
possibly private papers, hidden away somewhere
in her own old house. Where she lived for donkeys'
years. Where I am trying to exist now." He shot me
a rapid glance rather like an animal looking round.

"In short, I am treasure-hunting; and there's interference. That's the situation, naked and a bit ashamed of it. But the really odd thing is—she knows it."

"Knows what?"

"She knows I am after the loot," he answered, "and cannot rest in her grave. Wait till you have seen her face my dear feller, then scoff, if you can. She was a secretive old cat and she hated bipeds. Soured, I suppose. And she never stirred out of her frowsy seclusion for nearly twenty years. And *now* —her poor Arthur left gasping—she is fully aware of what her old enemy is at. Of every move I make. It's a fight to—well, past 'the death between us'. And *she* is winning."

"But my dear Beverley . . ." I began.

"My dear Rubbish," he said, squeezing my arm. "I am as sane as you are—only a little jarred and piqued. Besides I am not dragging you out at this time of night on evidence as vague as all that. I'll give you positive proof. *Perhaps* you shall have some pickings!"

We came at length to a standstill before his antiquated inheritance. An ugly awkward house, it abutted sheer on to the pavement. A lamp shone palely on its walls, its few beautifully-proportioned windows; and it seemed, if possible, a little quieter behind its two bay-trees—more resigned to night— than even its darkened neighbours were. We went in, and Beverley with a candle led the way down a long corridor.

"The front room", he said, pointing back, "is the dining-room. There's nothing there—simply the odour of fifty years of lavendered cocoon; fifty years of seed-cake and sherry. But even to sit on, there alone, munching one's plebeian bread-and-cheese, is to become conscious—well, is to become *conscious*. In *here*, though, is the mystery."

We stood together in the doorway, peering beneath our candle into a low-pitched, silent, strangely-attractive and old-fashioned parlour. Everything within it, from its tarnished cornice to its little old parrot-green beaded footstool, was the accumulated record of one mind, one curious, solitary human individuality. And it was as silent and unresponsive as a clam.

"What a fascinating old lady!" I said.

"Yes," he answered in a low voice. "There she is!"

I turned in some confusion, but only to survey the oval painted portrait of Miss Lemieux herself. She was little, narrow, black-mittened, straight-nosed, becurled; and she encountered my eyes so keenly, darkly, tenaciously, that I began to sympathize with both antagonists.

"Now this is the problem," he said, making a long nose at it, and turning his back on the picture. "I searched the house last week from garret to cellar and intend to begin again. The doubloons, the diamonds, the documents are here somewhere, and as R.L.S. said in another connection, If she's *Hide*, then I'm Seek. On Sunday I came in here to have a think. I sat there, in that little chair, by the window staring vacantly in front of me, when presently in some indescribable fashion I became aware that I was being stared *at*." He touched the picture hanging up on its nail behind him with the back of his head. "So we sat, she and I, for about ten solid minutes, I should think. Then I tired of it. I turned the old Sphinx to the wall again, and went out. A little after nine I came back. There wasn't a whisper in the house. I had my supper, sat thinking again, and fell asleep. When I awoke, I was shivering cold.

I got up immediately, went out, shut the dining-room door with my face towards this one, went up a few stairs, my hand on the banister and then vaguely distinguished by the shadow that the door I had shut was ajar. I was certain I had shut it. I came back to investigate. And saw—*her*." He nodded towards the picture again. "I had left her as I supposed in disgrace, face to the wall: she had, it seemed, righted herself. But this may have been a mistake. So I deliberately took the old lady down from her ancestral nail and hid her peculiarly intent physiognomy in that cushion:

Dare not, wild heart, grow fonder!
Lie there, my love, lie yonder!

Then I locked windows, shutters and door and went to bed."

He paused and glanced at me out of the corner of his eye. "I dare say it sounds absurd," he said, "but next morning when I came down I dawdled about for at least half an hour before I felt impelled to open this door. The chair was empty. She was 'up'!"

"Any charwoman?" I ventured.

"On Tuesdays, Fridays and at the week-ends," he said.

"You are *sure* of it?" He looked vaguely at me, tired and protesting. "Oh, yes," he said, "last night's was my fifth experiment."

"And you want me . . . ?"

"Just to stay here and keep awake. *I can't.* That's all. Theorizing is charming—and easy. But the nights are short. You don't appear to have a vestige of nerves. Tell me who is playing this odd trick on me! Mind you, I *know* already. *Some*how it's this old She's who is responsible, who is manœuvring. But how?"

I exchanged a long look with him—with the cold blue gaze in the tired pallid face; then glanced back at the portrait. Into those small, feminine, dauntless, ink-black eyes.

He turned away with a vague shrug of his shoulders. "Of course," he said coldly, "if you'd rather *not.*"

"Go to bed, Beverley," I answered, "I'll watch till morning. . . . We are, you say, absolutely alone in this house?"

"Physically, yes; absolutely alone. Apart from *that* old cat there is not so much as a mouse stirring."

"No rival heirs? No positive claimants?"

"None," he said. "Though, of course. . . . It's only—my aunt." We stood in silence.

"Well, good night, then; but honestly I am rather sceptical."

He raised his eyebrows, faintly smiled—something between derision and relief, lifted the portrait from the wall, carried it across the room, leaned it against the armchair in the corner. "There!" he muttered. "Check! you old witch! . . . It's very good of you. I'm sick of it. It has relieved me immensely. Good night!" He went out quickly, leaving the door ajar. I heard him go up the stairs, and presently another door, above, slammed.

I thought at first how few candles stood between me and darkness. It was now too late to look for more. Not, of course, that I felt any real alarm. Only a kind of curiosity—that might perhaps leap into something a little different when off its guard! I sat down and began meditating on Beverley, his nerves, his pretences, his venomous hatred of . . . well, what? Of a dozen things. But beneath all this I was gazing in imagination straight into the pictured eyes of a little old lady, already months in her grave.

The hours passed slowly. I changed from chair to chair—"t.e.g." gift-books, albums of fading photographs, old picture magazines. I pored over some marvellously fine needlework, and a few enchanting little water-colours. My candle languished; its successor was kindled. I was already become cold, dull, sleepy and depressed, when in the extreme silence I heard the rustling of silk. Screening my candle with my hand, I sat far back into my old yellow damask sofa. Slow, shuffling footsteps were quietly drawing near. I fixed my eyes on the door. A pale light beyond

it began stealing inwards, mingling with mine.
Faint shadows zigzagged across the low ceiling.
The door opened wider, stealthily, and a most extraordinary figure discovered itself, and paused on
the threshold.

For an instant I hesitated, my heart thumping at
my ribs; and then I recognized, beneath a fantastic
disguise, no less tangible an interloper than Beverley
himself. He was in his pyjamas; his feet were bare;
but thrown over his shoulders was an immense old
cashmere shawl that might have once graced Prince
Albert's Exhibition in the Crystal Palace. And his
head was swathed in what seemed to be some preposterous eighteenth-century night-gear. The other
hand outstretched, he was carrying his candlestick a
few inches from his face, so that I could see his every
feature with exquisite distinctness beneath his voluminous head-dress.

It was Beverley right enough—I noticed even a
very faint likeness to his brother, Henry, unperceived till then. His pale eyes were wide and glassily
open. But behind this face, as from out of a mask—
keen, wizened, immensely absorbed—peered his
little old enemy's unmistakable visage, Miss Lemieux's! He was in a profound sleep, there could be no
doubt of that. So closely burned the flame to his
entranced face I feared he would presently be setting
himself on fire. He moved past me slowly with an
odd jerky constricted gait, something like that of a
very old lady. He was muttering, too, in an aggrieved queer far-away voice. Stooping with a sigh,

he picked up the picture; returned across the room; drew up and mounted the parrot-green footstool, and groped for the nail in the wall not six inches above his head. At length he succeeded in finding it; sighed again and turned meditatively; his voice rising a little shrill, as if in altercation. Once more he passed me by unheeded and came to a standstill; for a moment, peering through curtains a few inches withdrawn, into the starry garden. Whether the odd consciousness within him was aware of *me*, I cannot say. Those unspeculating, window-like eyes turned themselves full on me crouched there in the yellow sofa. The voice fell to a whisper; I think that he hastened a little. He went out and closed the door, and I'd swear my candle solemnly ducked when his was gone!

I huddled myself up again, pulled up a rug and woke to find the candle-stub still alight in the dusk of dawn—battling faintly together to illuminate the little vivid painted face leaning from the wall. And that, on my soul—showing not a symptom of fatigue —in this delicate Spring daybreak, indeed appeared more redoubtable than ever!

I sat for a time undecided what to be doing, what even to be thinking. And then, as if impelled by an inspiration, I got up, took down again the trophy from its nail, and with my pen-knife gently prized open the back of its gilded frame. Surely, it had occurred to me, it could not be mere vanity, mere caprice or rancour that could take such posthumous pains as this! Perhaps, ever dimly aware of it as he was in his waking moments, merely the pressing sub-conscious thought of the portrait had lured Beverley out of his sleep. Perhaps . . .

I levered up the thin dusty wood; there was nothing beneath. I drew it out from the frame. And then was revealed, lightly pasted on the back, a scrap of yellowed paper, scrawled with five crosses in the form of a quincunx. In one corner of this was a large, capital Italianate "P". And beneath a central cross was drawn a small square. Here was the veritable answer before my eyes. How very like old age to doubt its memory even on such a crucial matter as this. Or was it only doubt?

For whose guidance had this odd quincunx been intended? Not for Walter Beverley's—that was certain. Standing even where I was I could see between the curtains the orchard behind the house pale in the dawn with its fast-fading fruit-blossom. There, then, lay concealed the old lady's secret "hoard". We had but to exercise a little thought, a little dexterity and precaution; and Beverley had won.

And then suddenly, impetuously, rose up in my mind an obstinate distaste of meddling in the matter. Surely, if there is any such thing as desecration, *this* would be desecration.

I glanced at the old attentive face looking up at me, the face of one who had, it seemed, so easily betrayed her most intimate secret, and in some unaccountable fashion there now appeared to be something quite other than mere malice in its concentration—a hint even of the apprehension and entreaty

of a heart too proud to let them break through the
veil of the small black fearless eyes.

I determined to say nothing to Beverley; watch
yet again. And—if I could find a chance—dig by
myself, and make sure of the actual contents of Miss
Lemieux's treasury before surrendering it to her
greedy, insensitive heir. So once more the portrait
was re-hung on its rusty nail.

He was prepared for my scepticism; but he did
not believe, I think, that I had kept unceasing
watch.

"I am sure," he said repeatedly, "absolutely sure
that what I told you last night has recurred repeatedly. How can you disprove my positive personal evidence by this one failure—by a million
negatives? It is you who are to blame—that tough,
bigoted *common* sense of yours."

I willingly accepted his verdict and offered to
watch once more. He seemed content. And yet by
his incessant restlessness and the curious questioning
dismay that haunted his face I felt that his nocturnal
guest was troubling and fretting him more than
ever.

It was a charming old house, intensely still, intensely self-centred, as it were. One could imagine
how unwelcome the summons of death would be in
such a familiar home on earth as this. I wandered,
and brooded, and searched in the garden: and found
at length without much difficulty my "quincunx".
The orchard was full of fruit trees, cherry, plum,
apple: but the five towering pear trees, their rusty

crusted bloom not yet all shed, might become at once unmistakably conspicuous to anyone in possession of the clue; though not till then. But how hopeless a contest had my friend set himself with no guidance, and one spade, against such an aunt, against such an orchard!

Evening began to narrow in the skies. My host and I sat together over a bottle of wine. Much as he seemed to cling to my company, I knew he longed for solitude. Twice he rose, as if urged by some sudden caprice to leave me, and twice he sat down again in even deeper constraint.

But soon after midnight I was left once more to my vigil. This time I forestalled his uneasy errand and replaced the portrait myself. I rested awhile; then, when it was still very early morning, I ventured out into the mists of the garden to find a spade. But I had foolishly forgotten on which side of the mid-most tree Miss Lemieux had set her tell-tale square. So back again I was compelled to go, and this time I took the flimsy, precious scrap of paper with me. Somewhere a waning moon was shedding light, for the mists of the garden were white as milk and the trees stood phantom-like above the drenched grasses.

I pinned the paper to the mid-most pear tree, measured out with my eye a rough narrow oblong a foot or two from the trunk and drove the rusty spade into the soil.

At that instant I heard a cautious minute sound behind me. I turned and once more confronted the pathetic bedizened figure of the night before. It was fumbling with the handle of the window, holding aloft a candle. The window opened at length and Beverley stood peering out into the garden. I fancied even a shrill voice called. And then without hesitation, with the same odd, shuffling gait Beverley stepped out on to the dew-damped gravel path and came groping towards me. He stood then, quietly watching me, not two paces distant; and so utterly still was the twilight that his candle-flame burned slim and unwavering in the mist, shedding its small, pale light on leaf-sprouting flowerless bough and dewdrop, and upon that strange set haunted face.

I could not gaze very long into the grey unseeing eyes. His lips moved. His fingers, oddly bent, twitched. And then he turned from me. The large pale eyes wandered to my spade, to the untrampled grasses, and finally, suddenly fixed their gaze on the tiny square of fading paper. He uttered a little cry, shrill and desperate, and stretched out his hand to snatch it. But I was too quick for him. Doubling it up, I thrust it into my pocket and stepped back beneath the trees. Then, intensely anxious not to awaken the sleep-walker, I drew back with extreme caution. None the less, I soon perceived that, however gradual my retreat, he was no less patiently driving me into a little shrubbery where there would be no chance of eluding him, and we should stand confronting one another face to face.

I could not risk a struggle in such circumstances. A wave of heat spread over me; I tripped, and then ran as fast as I could back to the house, hastened into the room and threw myself down in my old yellow sleeping-place—closing my eyes as if I were lost to the world. Presently followed the same faint footfall near at hand. Then, hearing no sound at all, and supposing he had passed, I cautiously opened my eyes—only to gaze once more unfathomably deep into his, stooping in the light of his candle, searching my face insanely, entreatingly—I cannot describe with how profound a disquietude.

I did not stir, until, with a deep sigh, like that of a tired-out child, he turned from me and left the room.

I waited awhile, my thoughts like a disturbed nest of ants. What should I do? To whom was my duty obligatory?—to Beverley, feverishly hunting for wealth not his (even if it existed) by else than earthly right; or to this unquiet spirit—that I could not but believe had taken possession of him—struggling, only *I* knew how bravely, piteously and desperately, to keep secret—what? Not mere money or valuables or private papers or personal secrets which might lie hidden beneath the shadow of the pear tree. Surely never had eyes pleaded more patiently and intensely and less covetously for a stranger's chivalry, nor from a wilder ambush than these that had but just now gazed into mine. What was the secret; what lure was detaining on earth a shade so much in need of rest?

I took the paper from my pocket. Light was swiftly flowing into the awakening garden. A distant thrush broke faintly into song. Undecided—

battling between curiosity and pity, between loyalty to my friend and loyalty to even *more* than a friend —to this friendless old woman's solitary perturbed spirit, I stood with vacant eyes upon the brightening orchard—my back turned on portrait and room.

A hand (no *man's* asleep, or awake) touched mine. I turned—debated no more. The poor jaded face was grey and drawn. He seemed himself to be inwardly wrestling—possessed against possessor. And still the old bygone eyes within his own, across how deep an abyss, argued, pleaded with mine. They seemed to snare me, to persuade me beyond denial. I held out the flimsy paper between finger and thumb.

Like the limb of an automaton, Beverley's arm slowly raised his guttering candle. The flame flowed soft and blue. I held the paper till its heat scorched my thumb. Something changed; something but just now there was suddenly gone. The old, drawn face melted, as it were, into another. And Beverley's voice broke out inarticulate and feverish. I sat him down and let him slowly awaken. He stared incredulously to and fro, from the window to me, to the portrait, and at last his eye fell on his extraordinary attire.

"I say," he said, "what's this?"

"Seemingly," I said, "they are the weeds of the malevolent aunt who has been giving you troubled nights."

"Me?" he said, not yet quite free from sleep.

"Yes," I said.

He yawned. "Then—I have been fooled?" he said.

174

I nodded. I think that even tears came into his eyes. The May-morning choragium of the wild birds had begun, every singer seemingly a soloist in the enraptured medley of voices.

"Well, look here!" he said, nodding a stupid sleep-drowsed head at me, "look here! What . . . you think of an aunt who hates a fellow as much as that, eh? What you think?"

"I don't know what to think," I said.

AN ANNIVERSARY

At least a minute—and one that resembled not only a sort of hole in Time but a pause in eternity—must have ticked its moments away; but even yet Aubrey could not be positively certain of what he had seen. Of the after effects of just that one transfixed vague glimpse, his present attitude—long-chinned face thrust forward; cold, grey, light-lashed eyes peering fixedly through the budding tresses of his contorted weeping-ash—was evidence enough.

His earthenware pitcher still dangled from his numbed fingers. The blood in his throat and temples continued its faint drumming, and was the cause perhaps of the peculiar descending shimmer, as of motes of light, that now affected his vision. His eyes themselves, it seemed, had refused to let him make sure. He had been abjectly shaken—momentarily terrified even. The scalp on his head was still tingling. And yet he had continued to think.

He had made a habit of attending to what happened "in his mind", and was well aware that unpleasing memories, if they are steadily suppressed and driven down into the dark of that mind, may yet somehow grope to the surface again and re-appear in unexpected disguises. Especially when one is not "watching-out" for them! What then of this particular memory?

For a whole year it had stationed itself like a skulking menacing shadow on the outskirts of consciousness. With anything so habitual one does not even have to look to see if it is still there; just as in one's own house—at the end perhaps of a corridor, or on the landing of a staircase, may hang a portrait which appears as if what it represented were always steadily in wait for—well, for a renewed and really close scrutiny of itself.

And even though faces in portraits are only made of paint on canvas, they can yet shed on one a sort of passive influence.

The inward shade that frequented Aubrey's mind was not however a mere portrait. It was the vivid mental image of a "friend" whom he had sufficient reason to distrust, and even detest, although its original must long ago, surely, have given up all earthly (or any other) concern with him. Or with Emily, either! The bourne from which, please God, no traveller returns—.It had needed no Shakespeare to discover that! Why then quite unexpectedly—not out of the blue, perhaps—but out of these cold evening shadows had . . . ? That was the question. A fantastic yet rather pressing question. What neglect there had been up to the present, had, it is true, been on one side only. The friend's. Not on Aubrey's. And he

believed that he knew all that he needed to know of
Emily.

When two minds, a man's and a woman's, are in
close and frequent association with one another—or
two bodies for that matter—each, it seems, may be
silently aware even of what may be secretly passing
in the other's. They seem to play eavesdropper, not
only to one another's thoughts but even sensations.
But then, women are assumed to be more sentimental than men. More sentimental at any rate than
Aubrey was himself by nature, or than he had any
intention of being. Over anniversaries, for example
—birthdays, wedding-days, red-letter days, promise-
days, love-days, mothers'-days, death-days. It was
fantastic. It was as if their hearts were their calendars
—dismally trustworthy calendars in the clearest of
print. To let the dead past bury not only its dead
but also its moribund, and bury it deep, had always
been—by much—Aubrey's private preference.

And what of that sinister and secretive evil jealousy? Which may rot into a wearisome and corro-
sive hatred. Hack away as you will at its roots and
suckers they will begin sprouting again even in the
small hours of a single night. They become en-
tangled with the instincts, and are the hops and
brambles and bindweed of the imagination. Trailing,
tender, almond-scented bindweed—Aubrey had
read somewhere—will penetrate into loamy churchyard sod and soil a sheer nine feet. "Full fathom
five." But that *he* should have fallen a prey to
jealousy! And with nothing but envy and a worn-

out passion, no affection even, for its justification!

Apart from any reasons, however—and hatred no more than love positively needs any—he had at first sight taken a sudden hatred to John Fiske. In the whole wide world he was certain there was nothing they could have ever agreed about. "Oil and vine-gar," yes; but here there had been no salad. One can sneer at, despise, and label an enemy stupid and stolid, too, and yet realize that it would be nearer the mark if in the latter epithet one omitted the "t". In spite of his cursed "honesty", his stubborn directness and unshakable devotion (to what did not belong to him), John Fiske had been as hard to see through as he had been to explore. More im-penetrable indeed even than the gloom now steadily deepening beneath the branches of this weeping-ash.

Besides, Aubrey had been envious of Fiske long before he had become jealous of him. Not because he thought him as quick and clever—and certainly not as attractive—as himself. It was his dull, suety, habitually good qualities that he abominated most. They can be the very devil when one wants the owner of them out of the way. As for his own good qualities—brains, morals, heart? He'd have given himself a *plus* for the first. And the rest? Well, according to taste! Also he knew what he wanted. As, of course, in his slow, honest-to-god, nauseating fashion had Fiske. Precisely how much of his own particular *want* had he got? By no means all; Aubrey himself had seen to that. And yet . . . to hell with him!

There, indeed, so far as undertaker, sexton, and the passing of time can manage, was precisely where he might perhaps be now; and for good! Though, somehow, the clever seem to be its likelier inhabitants. Why on earth then was he himself dithering about like this, outside this arboreal cage, and extremely reluctant to venture into it? Solely because it had for that split second seemed to be *occupied*; and by a vigilant and tongueless intruder loafing in wait by a damp-greened old water-butt—his clock a dripping tap!

Aubrey's first symptoms of shock having now subsided, one simple question presented itself. Since what he had seen, or had appeared to see, could by no possibility be actual—not at any rate as actual as the water-butt—could it have been "real"? If real, it would prove a deadly nuisance, and might entail the vilest complications. If not real, it had been merely an illusion.

"Ghosts"—pah! No, from that bourne *no* traveller returns; and that may be damned bad luck for those beyond it! "Dead men rise up never"; no matter into what Dead Sea even the weariest river may eventually wind its way. Apart from their bones and their worldly chattels the only thing the dead leave behind them is their memory. But that—such is the imbecility of the human mind—however anxiously it is hidden, may, as Emily would agree, become an obsession. And obsessions may breed illusions. With *them*, bell, book and candle are of far less service than *pot. brom.* A sneer webbed over Aubrey's cold stiff features. For, with Emily, even *pot. brom.*, let alone her Evening Services, tame-cattiness and deadly taciturnity, had failed.

Real or not, it was just like Fiske to have chosen this particular place and time for—well, this re-union. During the lingering days of autumn how often at his work in the City used Aubrey's fascin-ated fancy to turn to this last half-hour of twilight in his long straggling garden; these motionless, misty, earthy, early October evenings, the last of the sunset withering in the west. He loved the reek of his leaf bonfires and its haunting nutty odour of decay. He loved being alone; or, rather perhaps, being in strict privacy. And here, even at noonday, his garden was screened from the direct scrutiny of his neighbours. He was a person who refused not only to allow himself to be neglected, but also to be overlooked. But there are eyes that, once met, cannot even in memory be disregarded.

Apart from direct access by way of the house, the only route into and out of Aubrey's garden lay through a wicket-gate that led into the open—into wide, flat and now mist-bound fields of damp and malodorous cabbages and cauliflowers, sour acres and acres of deserted market gardens. Yet back from his day in London, he delighted in pottering and, hardly less, in pretending to potter. A perpetual and pleasing activity of mind usually accompanied this busy dolittle. He was abnormally secretive. For

weeks he had held his tongue while that little romance of "yesteryear" had steadily intensified and
his own particular little intentions and designs had
no less steadily matured. And even this no doubt was
in part because of his peculiar pleasure in his own
society; even at its worst. He especially enjoyed a
festering stagnant mood. Not that many human
beings are not pleasanter when they are alone. It is
an eventuality that may be of equal advantage to
their friends.

Indeed, who would deny that it is chiefly the presence of one's fellow-creatures that evokes one's
worst—though these may possibly be one's rarest—
characteristics! Alone, even by no means virtuous
people may mean wholly well. Not so Aubrey. He
despised what he called cant; and first and foremost
he *meant* business. It was, too, in the solitude of his
garden, particularly as dusk thickened, that he could
best explore his little plans. Then, as if with a dark
lantern, he could follow up the wavering intersecting
paths leading into the future. Digging, trenching,
and even weeding, helped him to concentrate. He
was something of a sapper, too; sly and sedulous
when things or people stood in his way.

But why so thirsty a creature? He delighted in cold
water especially and drank large quantities of it. For
one thing, it was all but free. For another one's wet
may be a trifle too dry. It was, then, a special
pleasure—his gardening done for the day—to sally
off down to the water-butt under his weeping-ash,
and there fill his earthenware pitcher. For himself,

and for the flowers and pot-plants indoors. It was due, perhaps, to the Old Adam in him, after the fall of Eve. Also he had a nice taste in flowers. One might almost describe him as an intellectual aesthete who, on his arrival into this unrighteous world, had been deprived of a suitable start.

As this very moment, he stood listening, he could hear from under the tree the furtive falling sing-song of the waterdrops out of the pump's iron spout—a tuneless tune, either entirely heedless of its surroundings, or, contrariwise, endeavouring to warn him of something amiss. But what? Just lately, as the days drew in, it had been more than dusk, it had been all but dark, when he had abandoned his flower-beds. The first stars would be pricking into the sky. He would stand, looking up; amused to remind himself that these sparkling darlings of the poets and sentimentalists are nothing but remote and unimaginably immense vats of gas or "energy"— anything you please, except the pretty-pretty. That, beyond inconceivably icy Saharas of pitch-black space, they are not only at some appalling velocity hastening towards (or was it away from?) man's silly little solar system, but are also running *down*! It was an anarchistic little notion that made him laugh. *All* of us, every one of us, doomed! What concern had they indeed with human affairs?—these celestial glow-worms, devoid even of harbouring a consciousness! His *own* "star" was quite another matter. That was *his* concern; or, at any rate, he meant to make it so.

An Anniversary

And now, large as life, as reserved, as unfathomable, and—damn his eyes—as coldly contemptuous of Aubrey himself as ever, here was this devil, Fiske —or his double, or his revenant, his astral body or mere presentment, masquerading in the shelter of Aubrey's very own private weeping-ash!

"Come back," had he! What for? *Whom* for? Ah, yes! In that maze we call the mind (and heart too), even an illusion may have a purpose and a motive, though either may remain securely hidden in the unconscious. If this was solely his own illusion and he himself was its only goal, well and good. But suppose Emily . . . ? No, he badly needed that there should be no meddling with her. Not yet, anyhow. And to confess to an illusion! *To her!*

He realized that he was being compelled to pay attention to a mere trick of the senses, to a silly hallucination—which might none the less tend to become a habitual hallucination. With the advent of this abused notion, Aubrey suddenly changed his mind. A brilliant idea! Why *not* presently make mocking mention to Emily of this silly illusion— and watch *her* reactions. It would all sound so plausible, and so natural, and so harmless. . . . "Yes, darling, just now. As a matter of fact—having finished up—I was just going indoors to fill the water-pot when. . . ."

There had been too much futile reserve and concealment during these last months—the first vindictive indictments and persecutions over and before stagnancy had set in. Far better perhaps bring the whole stupid business into the open again. Yes, and keep it there. If his fancies intended to prey on him, they might in that case not have to prey for very long. Every female heart has its snapping-point. The elastic perishes.

What need then was there for worry? Solely and solidly, of course, because all this entailed a crucial little question of £.s.d. "Ghosts", whatever their texture, may gibber; but *money* talks. And loudly too, if one has the need or the desire to listen. Had Emily, or had she not, made another Will? If she had, then, he could be practically certain of disaster. And for the life of him he could not conceive of any hiding-place as yet unattended to. Not at least in the house. If she had not; well, better not inquire too closely. In any case she had not forgotten.

That covertly scrutinized tell-tale face! The lurking shadows, the hauntedness beneath those rounded eyelids, had never left it. Neither by day nor by night had it lost either its pallor or its settled melancholy. An abandoned Ophelia, suckling a secret so intense and so profound. Those long lapses too into silence and vacancy. Recently he had done his level best to let this particular sleeping dog lie. And in so doing how much he had missed the amusing but now forbidden sport of stirring its maudlin slumbers. Passive resistance, passive acceptance—which was the most galling? He had begun to fancy, moreover, that slander—or intuition—had been busy with his own little activities.

Supposing, then, that, after all, with her pestilent

mother for accomplice, Emily was debating, still in doubt, whether or not to leave him? No guile, no subtlety, not even his own, could extort so much as a nod from her on that. Was she herself less candid, less transparent than he had supposed? Well, she had discovered long ago what kind of fish she had netted; or been netted by. Why, then, was he fudging and faltering like this?

There had been a light rain that evening, gently weeping clouds; and only at this moment had he become aware that a newish moon was sinking in the west—a moon well on her way to her first quarter, faintly silvering the ash twigs, vaguely adulterating the gloom within. How easily might his recent little experience have been a pure deceit? And yet, could the mere misconception of some familiar object have continued active for so long? How many moments—minutes—had he been caught up in this idiotic trance?

Aubrey stooped a little, shut his eyes very tight for a few instants, then opened them again. Idiot! The effort had only made them less effective. Those scintillant luminous motes poured softly on.

At length, lifting his left hand—as gently as a Gehazi peering in upon an Elisha—he drew a fan of twigs an inch or two aside.

"Well!" he heard his dry lips calling softly into the gloom. "What about it, then? . . . Is that you, Fiske?"

In the complete history of mankind never surely

had a more imbecile question been addressed into a
silence so intent. Not a single syllable of this dramatic
little adjuration had been consciously present in his
mind until he had heard his own voice utter it. A
queer voice too. And no wonder. There, in every
obscure detail, utterly motionless, mutely and tran-
quilly challenging, the illusion had taken shape
again—or in the interval had remained unaffected.
There was no active speculation in those eyes—nor
assuredly anything approaching a "glare". They
were still faintly luminous and serenely inquiring,
as if in some remote meditation. At this overwhelming proof of his beastly predicament, provoked too
perhaps by the shaken and muffled tones of his own
voice and the effort to stop his teeth chattering,
Aubrey's wits had become slightly unbalanced. He
stooped lower; coughed. He was afraid.

"Whoever you are, *what*ever you are," he heard
his swollen tongue declare, "you have no bloody
business to be here. Understand that! You——! If
you want me—or anybody else, for that matter—
you know where the gate is, and you can go round
to the front. Do you hear me? Go round to the
front, curse you; and knock like a gentleman!"

But had he in fact uttered these words? Or had he
only overheard one of those inward interlopers who
begin so garrulously shouting into one's ear on the
very brink of sleep? He had, at any rate, *thought*
them; and the rebuke had done something to restore
his confidence. He knew—oh, absolutely—that no
answer would come. He defied an answer. Indeed,

the only perceptible change in his surroundings—
the faintest of changes—was that the deepening
darkness into which he was peering had been very
feebly diminished. As cautiously as an animal venom-
ously resentful of its cage he glanced over his
shoulder. Well, he had bidden his visitor go round
to the front and knock; and knock like a gentleman.
And now, as if for a symbol of how warmly he
would be welcomed, a light which must momentarily have shone out and down from an upper window of the house behind him, had suddenly gone
out. Its walls and windows—its whole presence now
blank again as a sepulchre's.

This time, too, when he himself wheeled swiftly
round again, there was absolutely nothing to be seen
but his mute own familiar pump beneath its writhen
wattled tent of intertwining ash-boughs.

And a silence had fallen, curdled only by that one
tiny monotonous watery whimper, intent not only
on repeating the same tune on and on and over and
over again, but on *singing* it! God help him! Coun-
terfeit or not, the "Black Man" had certainly taken
shape. The shape of Fiske.

And, although Aubrey's lean, long-chinned face,
his pale eyes and brass-coloured hair hardly suggested that he was likely to be the victim of nerves,
this precisely was what he was in danger of now.
. . . And for how long? He swallowed the hoarse
laugh of bravado that had slid into his throat before
it had become audible, and for yet another moment
or two still hesitated to intrude, from out of the

open, into the little tent of darkness that until this evening had been his all but unfailingly happy heritage as tenant of his garden. What the eye cannot see, the skin may become aware of! Still, go right in he did at last, and waited until his pitcher was three parts full, striving the while to breathe less quickly the dank autumnal air, and to slow up his silly heartbeats. He was alone now, acutely so. His visitor, his visitant, had absconded. But never never again would his idolized garden be able to convince him that his solitude was absolute and complete.

The mists from the rain-soaked flats beyond his wicket-gate were now not only visible but smellable and tasteable. Whereas his late visitant—well, he could not say what precise conspiracy of his senses had been responsible for *him*. He had assuredly not been audible. "So much for that!" Aubrey muttered to himself, as he gave a violent wrench to the cold water-wet tap in the hope of silencing its silly, officious, doll-like musical box. "Now for the rest of the play!" He even regretted he had not reminded his meddlesome enemy that there was a notice-board at the gate out of the market-gardens proclaiming: "No Admittance: except on Business."

The faint tinkle of a bell sounded from the house behind him. He swore under his breath. "That's just what these idiots *would* be doing at such a moment." And as yet he had had no time for a wash or to change his gardening boots—clumpers, half an inch thick with sodden soil. He took out his handkerchief and wiped his face and head. He was exhausted, solely by the strain of standing motionless, for, perhaps, three complete minutes! Or was it months? He must go in; and quickly. A cold, jagged smile broke over his features. Supposing that a little while ago, he had been taken at his word! A rat-tat-tat-tat? . . . *Qui vive?* . . . Who knows? And what then?

Or had what happened in the solitude of the garden been only a novel and beastly symptom of one of his own familiar little attacks? Yet another bout—and as early as October? A glimpse of himself, feeble and sweating on a sick-bed, swam into his view. How much he loathed repeated, parrot-like inquiries and that evening-tray laden with its tail-swallowed whiting, or insipid minced chicken, and miniature "light pudding". Or tapioca! That would be when he was getting better. Getting better, yes: but then, you never knew!

However, he was no weakling. He had schooled himself in the past to face what may come, and particularly if he had arranged for it. Dunning letters, for example; plea-ful letters; indiscreet, passionate, aggrieved outpourings of the heart; rate-collectors; and now and then the moneylender's jackal. Just wait! And above all, keep calm! Think before you speak. Watch! And never never—unless you are positively cornered—never lose your temper or your balance.

Unless, in the next world, space is of no consequence, unless time is non-existent in eternity, it would take his *revenant*, his come-back, his spook, if not his hallucination, at least ten minutes to get round from his garden gate to the front door. Why, he wondered, must the thought of a slow but sure walking apparition be so much less savoury in the fancy, than, say, the classic method devised for its reappearance by the usual medium? A Fiske consisting of ectoplasm! And why was he himself *still* listening? The squeal of his front gate could be heard a mile off. But had he shut it? What the hell was the use of asking himself such fatuous questions?

He pushed back his handkerchief into his pocket, lifted his pitcher of well-water—twice as heavy as it had ever been before—trod steadily and stealthily back to the house, set it down on the stones in the back porch, opened the door and went in.

The fusty room beyond, although it contained his pet primulas and gloxinias, was scarcely worthy of being called a conservatory, and there was only darkness now to see his treasures by; so that, when he opened the french window and pushed back the curtain that concealed the dining-room beyond, the instantaneous electric blaze for the instant all but blinded him. It was as sudden as a blow in the face.

The room was vacant; but everything lay ready on the table and on the sideboard, flowers, china, silver, shining and twinkling there, mute and peaceful. "Still life!" He glanced at the clock on the chimney-piece—a wedding present. It at once began to tick. He went softly in, then out into the demure-scrupulously clean and garnished little "hall" beyond. Fingers and thumb on the newel of its post, he paused at the foot of the staircase.

And, as if he had been heard listening—"Oh! Is that you, Aubrey? Supper's ready," a voice called faintly from upstairs. "I am just coming. I was getting a handkerchief."

"Right, darling!" he shouted back, but louder than he had intended. "But don't come down. I am coming up. I must have a wash. I was kept in the garden. I mean I could not get . . ."

" 'Kept in the garden'?" echoed the voice, a little nearer now, and even as if the owner of it were awaiting, even dreading, what so simple an explanation might mean, although he had carefully refrained from making it unusual by even a fraction of a syllable.

"Don't come down," he repeated. "I am coming up—this moment." He paused to swallow. "Everything all right?" Dam' fool!

"Oh, very well," came the answer, yet faintlier. "Yes, everything. I shall be in the bathroom. I am getting a hot-water bottle."

A hot-water bottle! The old self-pampering! More invalidism—and doctors' bills. The old "pains", he supposed. But surely she couldn't be going to bed! "Clay—clay-cold is my earthy mouth". . . . How *did* the old borderland jingle go?

Treading with an almost cat-like punctilio on the mats, from door to door, with two almost soundless intervening steps on the linoleum between them, he made his way into the kitchen. All that for the

moment he could see of its only inmate was a hum-
mock of black skirts, a strip of what appeared to be
a petticoat, and exposed heels. The rest of her was
concealed by the open door of the gas oven.

"Mary," he cried softly. "Don't dish up just yet.
I am not ready. And——"

A long, dark and intent face had made its appearance above the oven door.

"What I was going to say", he explained, "is that
—well, there *may* be a visitor. And I don't want Mrs.
Silcot to be worried just now. She seems to be over-
tired."

Yet again he listened to an ejected statement that
he could have taken his Bible oath he had never
meant to make. Well, he must stick to it.

The dark stare from above the oven door had
intensified. Sullen rat! Who paid her wages?

"A visitor! . . . Staying for supper!"

"Yes. Oh, no. I didn't mean that. Only that if
anyone should knock whom you may not recognize
—don't *necessarily* ask him in. I see there is no light
in the hall yet; I'll switch that on first. It may, of
course, be nothing at all; merely a false alarm. I
mean, of course, there's only a possibility. . . . In the
City this afternoon. . . ."

Why had the stolid colourless face stirred not so
much as an eyelid? Merely stared?

"I mean," he fumbled on, "if no one comes, it
does not matter. Obviously. There is no need to
wait about, I mean; except *not* to dish up for the
time being. But, if so—*if* anyone should—then just

N   193

come to *me*, and say, 'A Mr. Hamilton wishes to see you. It's about a picture." Something of that kind. I am not suggesting, mind"—and an all but winsome smile edged into his grey features—"that it *will* be a Mr. Hamilton. Or about a picture. It might be somebody else. However, that will be all right. *I* shall understand. Do you see what I mean?"

Mary abruptly turned her head away; paused, as it seemed, to exchange a few words with the interior of the oven; then rose to her feet. She then firmly shut-to the oven door. She knew that she had been watching him more intently than was necessary while he had given his directions, his "orders". But then you can never be sure what some people are up to. *That* rigmarole!—and a face like a half-starved ferret. She looked at him again point-blank, with her pitch-black, disciplined eyes. A bleak, plain, honest stare; and intelligent.

"Very good, sir," she said. "You don't know whether or not. But *if* so, a Mr. Hamilton. I quite understand. But nobody extra. And whoever it is, I am to say, 'a Mr. Hamilton' . . . Mrs. Silcot is poorly again?"

"Ah," Aubrey answered the tone of her remark, not its meaning. "Yes, I am sorry."

Yet again his rasp-edged temper had nearly got the better of him. Of what consequence was it what a servant thought or felt? No *love* was lost between them! Let her do as she was told, or get out. Even Emily would agree to that. Or would she? Even the dustman was a devotee of Emily's. As quietly as if he were a strange cat in his own house he turned away from the kitchen and its hated inmate and mounted the stairs. Arrived at the bathroom, he paused at the open door, watching for a while Emily bathed in the bright electric light within, as she stood, head thrown back, gargling over the basin.

"What's wrong now?" he inquired.

"Oh!" said Emily, ejecting the mouth-wash. "It's this geyser. It takes such an age to heat up. I thought I would have my bath a little earlier than usual."

"That, darling, is because you never manage it right," he retorted. "And anyhow it's better than getting the water scalding hot out of the tap before you can say knife. What I really meant was—not so much the tap as—what's the matter with *you*?"

"Matter?" she echoed, glancing apprehensively over her shoulder. "I didn't say anything was the matter, Aubrey. Only I think I shall have to go to bed soon after supper. The same old thing."

"As I supposed," said Aubrey. And now her too-large luminous eyes had also suddenly become fixed on his fair pallid features. An ingenuous but searching scrutiny had met a viper-like stare in an instantaneous conflict of questioning. "After dinner eh?"

"What was it you called up to me about the garden just now? You look as white as a ghost. *You're* not ill, Aubrey?"

The mask had all but taken to itself the appearance of plaster of Paris. It had set so hard.

"That's merely your childish way of getting even;

of evasion, my dear. An old dodge!" he answered as sweetly as his mouth would let him. "I stumbled —fetching water in the garden. And anyhow, what are we waiting for? *Mary?* There is never—I say, *never*—a single meal in this house on the tick. And surely you aren't going to suggest that that has anything to do with the geyser?"

Emily paused a moment in the act of stooping to put down the kettle, and was now screwing in the stopper of the water bottle. She watched her fingers.

"The bell rang about five minutes ago," she said.

"Look here, Emily," Aubrey broke out, "it's not a particle of use your attempting to come down to dinner. You just sham that these aches and pains are of no importance, and so only make them worse. You are to go to bed *now*; and the janitrix shall bring you up something on a tray—some nice minced chicken, and a cup of cocoa, perhaps." He had listened to this idiotic irony, and his stomach had fallen. "Keep *friends!*" urged an inward voice.

Emily paused a second time. She had gradually fallen into the habit, during these last months, of thinking over every answer she was on the point of making to her husband— Before its terms became irretrievable.

"I am very sorry," she said at last. "But isn't that a little inconsistent? There can't be anything seriously 'wrong'. At least. . . . Of course there can't. And you have always said that it's best not to pay attention to such things. You have always said, 'Wait for them to make you do so.' There was only a little faintness. And—well, just here." But her left hand was already stationed over her breast-bone.

Almost as if an hour-glass hung suspended in the air before his eyes, Aubrey was watching the sands of time as they soundlessly glided away.

"First it was aches and pains," he argued. "Now it is 'a little faintness'. These women!

"And wasn't it *I*"—he had raised his voice a little —"wasn't it *I* who at last insisted on your seeing the doctor again? And wasn't it *I* who insisted on his sounding and ninety-nining you and flourishing that absurd rubber contraption in his ladylike fingers— careless devil? And didn't he *say* that he could find nothing organically wrong? Pah! 'Organically'! Good heavens, I had a heart for years—when I was a boy; and was not even taken off football. All that palaver! This vague haze of suggestion. 'Symptoms!' They invent complications; phobias, as *they* call them. It pays."

Emily had turned away, pretending still to be drying the dumb rubber mouth of her hot-water bottle with a towel. By biting her lips perhaps she could the better keep her mouth shut.

"Of course . . . I'll go at once. But honestly, there is no need."

Aubrey drew back—a little too much for it to have been instinctive—behind the door, as she closely passed him by.

"I never even uttered the word 'need'," he called after her, and then on second thoughts followed her

into her bedroom, pausing only a moment to dip
his head over the rail of the landing, though he
failed to catch a glimpse of the front door.

"*Ouff*," he grumbled. "One could dine off merely
the smell of the cooking in this house before tasting
a mouthful. *That* fool!"

Emily was already drawing the short curtains over
the windows. He watched her face intently as she
turned down the sheet of her bed. So slow and
laborious was every movement that it might have
been a sheet of lead. And at every turn, when she
hoped she was unobserved, she glanced back at him.
What was really wrong? she was meditating. What
was behind all this? When a man is tired and hungry
one has to hold one's tongue. Anyhow, it's best to,
however unfair and morose he may be. Yes, hold it
like a tactful, vigilant child—the child, thank God,
they were never going to have. And this time, like a
wicked child, *he* was complaining not because there
was anything to complain of, but because there was
not.

She folded the bedspread, lifted the bedclothes,
and pushed in the bottle between the sheets.

"There, now," she said, gingerly smiling round at
him, "that's all. But you know, Aubrey, how I hate
going to bed. Please don't let there be much on the
tray." She suppressed a faint shudder. "I am not
really hungry."

He hesitated. How the devil was he ever to get to
the point? Somewhere in the far dark of his mind he
had heard approaching footsteps faint as the coming

of feet on wool, like a man weightless as a shadow walking in snow. Snow!

"The fact is, Emily, what is really worrying and fretting you is the conviction that you ought to see a specialist. Then why—whatever apart from fees and humbug that blessed word implies, and it means of course having that wretched doctor back again— why don't you *say* so? I wish to God we had some- one we could depend on in this miserable neigh- bourhood." He paused again, watching her. "What, Emily, by the way, was the name of that fellow at Ambrey? A tall man, stiff as a board; with a nose and spectacles? *He* seemed to know his business."

Emily had sat down. She was stooping as if to draw off her shoe, and at this she fixed her eyes as intently on it as if the thing could speak.

"You mean Dr. McLechlan?"

"Yes, Dr. McLechlan. That's it. Dr. Mucklechk- chlan. Just like that! The snuffy Scotchman. You wouldn't, I suppose, like to see *him*?"

"But surely——" she paused. "Don't you remem- ber? He sold his practice nearly a year ago and went —wasn't it?—to Canada."

"Was it?" Aubrey continued to stare at his face in the looking-glass. Better, better, better to get down to brass tacks; to have it out. Just in case. And other things too. The dead past cannot always take care of itself—with the future in view.

"Canada, eh? That's a long way off. You have a remarkable memory for dates, Emily. You never, never forget. And yet, after all, it would be no great loss. Not now. He may have been clever; but he was a trifle underhanded, don't you think? Even fishy? But *his* friend? Don't you remember on the river that awful day in August when we sat in the boat under a bridge while the rusty rain dripped on and on into the salad? That seems a devil of a time ago. What was *his* name?"

She hadn't stirred. So that was it?—at last. Again! Not all omens prove false. "You *know* his name, Aubrey. You are only pretending. . . . You are stirring up. . . . Why?"

Aubrey watched himself laugh in the glass; though silent laughter more closely resembles a grimace. "Of course," he drawled, "I know his name. The 'Reverend' John Fiske. He *ought* of course to have gone into the Church. You agree to that? He might have some day become an archdeacon; gaiters and laced-up chapeau. In spite of the buns and oranges, it needs strong, silent men. Another anniversary, Emily! You had a very soft spot for him in that rebellious, susceptible heart of yours. Once. It was quite a dare."

Emily had at last managed to take off the second shoe, and had reached, with a shuddering sigh, for her bedroom slippers. Well, she must go on, she supposed.

"But . . . but what is the use, what is the purpose," she continued, "of pretence? Oh, heavens, haven't we had this all out again and again; ages, ages ago? You were talking of doctors. Dr. McLechlan was an excellent doctor."

"So it's to be 'All change'—for the time being?"

Aubrey inquired sarcastically. "I didn't say he was not a good doctor. I didn't even say that he was not an excellent doctor. But were *you* quite satisfied—afterwards? I have often wondered; though I don't remember to have mentioned it. But perhaps you hadn't much opportunity for thinking. Too far gone; stricken?"

"I refuse to ask or answer any more questions, Aubrey. Why, I mean, you have brought all this up again now. I should not have supposed that just mocking at anyone at . . . yes, at a grief like that, was. . . . But what I *am* asking now is, did you really have any doubt about Dr. McLechlan?"

"Well, you see, I happened to know Dr. McLechlan myself personally, and he talked the case over with me. Mockery, a quite natural little grievance, and all that aside, I never *wanted* to dig it up again. But if you must know, he told me himself that he had not really been satisfied. Regarding the result of his treatment of the case, I mean. And that *then* it was too late."

"Too late?"

"Yes, too late. And I—well, really, I didn't care a damn. Though, as a matter of fact, I was not so sure myself that I agreed with him."

" 'Agreed'?"

"My dear Emily, I do wish you would make an effort to get over the habit of just repeating every word one says. It's called cuckoo-ing. It gains time, of course. . . . I say, I didn't agree with him that it *was* too late."

"Then, did you tell him so? Did you? I want to know that." She bent still lower over her knees.

"*I*—tell him?" said her husband. "Certainly not. It is not for a mere layman to butt in—though that's what they lie in wait for. 'Tell *me* what's the matter with you, then I'LL tell *you*!'—That's their tack."

"You mean," she said, rising with a sigh of difficulty to her feet and facing him in the full light of the lamp over the dressing-table, scattered over with its shining glass, cosmetics and *gewgaws*, "you mean, *you* let it go? That it need not have been fatal—that he himself. . . . Oh, oh, I wish I were dead!" She flung her hands apart, and gazed steadily back at him. "But why do you ask *me*?"

" '*Me*?' " echoed he, in quiet derision. "Oh, I like that, and which 'he' may I ask? Why do I ask *her* about *him*? That's pretty good. I was right, however, about the soft spot. And, oh yes, I agree that we have discussed all this, or nearly all this before— and the precise quality of the softness. Nor, Emily, are you by any means the only person in this world who has ever wished herself dead. And in 'a better world', as they call it. But even from any kind of world some of us may now and then relent and come back again—alive-like, if not positively kicking. From 'the other side', I mean. Even to this. A very few. What I am really wanting to know, though— and please do try to be reasonable and calm about it —what I soberly and truly am pining to know is what would you do it—say, to-morrow evening—if I happened to meet our friend (*not* Dr. McLechlan), and I asked him home to supper with us?"

"After what you have said, Aubrey, and you don't seem to see, or even to suspect how awful it is about knowing and not saying whether or not Dr. McLechlan even suggested that he—that he need not have died. . . . No, I refuse to say anything more."

" 'She takes refuge in silence,' " Aubrey silently protested to the All-Highest. "And *that*", he added, "is just where, my dear, you are at last on the right tack. . . . So your precious Dr. McLechlan went off to Canada, did he? And if there was anything out of the common, a little mysterious; well, we can't ask him now, can we? No address. . . . In either case——"

"And I say to that", said Emily, "that not one of John's friends ever said a word that even suggested that. Anything 'mysterious', I mean."

"For heaven's sake don't keep niggling," said her husband. "It's just like a pretty pollie parrot. You will agree, you can't help agreeing, that you only had Dr. McLechlan's word for it. Actually. That his patient had just finally retired, I mean. We omitted attending the funeral, didn't we? You said that I somehow *made* you lose the train. Charitable. Besides, after all this time, why on earth should you mind so simple a question? Merely, if I *had* happened to meet the afflicted one, say, this afternoon? Well, *then*, good God, he couldn't be dead, could he? Though it might suggest that he was a bit restless? On the other hand does even an 'excellent' doctor never make mistakes? And especially if he wishes to do not merely one forlorn friend, but two, a little favour. You'll agree with me that that's an ingenious little suggestion. Even though I was gracious enough to accept him at his word. There is always that horrid little inquisition about one's having been in one's right mind. Still, a lie is a lie, even if there are grey and commendable ones as well as white. And just a word—a word that would finally put our friend John out of any needlessly unhappy thoughts concerning him, would certainly have been kind, and perhaps even condonable. For both your sakes."

Aubrey had ventured further into his own fantastic, pitiless trap than he had intended. His mouth remained ajar, in spite of his intention to shut it; and yet again he found himself listening, though his eyes, reflected in the quicksilver of the glass, continued to watch, as Emily came near. She even persuaded herself to lay a hand on his sleeve, to touch him.

"You are torturing me? You are beginning again? Well, even if—even if it should be for the last time. It was Dr. McLechlan himself who told me that you went to see him. That you even sat with John that afternoon of the very day before he—he died. Listen," her eyes were scrutinizing his face as though in search of what until this moment she could never so much as imagine could be discoverable there—discoverable even there. "Listen!" she repeated, "you *know* that you are hinting at what is absolutely untrue. You know that Dr. McLechlan did his very

best and. . . . Oh, I can't bear it. What has happened?
Something has *happened*, I say. Unless you want to
—well, to have done with me—you must tell me.
You will have to tell me."

"Oh-ho," Aubrey scarcely more than muttered
the words, breathing heavily, through distended
nostrils, "so now we are coming down to the naked
facts! Not very pleasant, either. So you couldn't
bear that little taradiddle, even now. Not even the
mere hypothesis. Strange, though, it never even
occurred to you. Wouldn't it have clinched the—
the . . . ? But there, Emily, husbands after all *will* be
husbands. You must have realized that long ago.
And Fiskes will be Fiskes. 'Fiskes!'—doesn't that
sound just awful? What kind of an animal, do you
think, would a Fiske resemble? No. No. I am *not*
questioning the death certificate. I was merely, well,
making up. But just to clear things up a little further,
more tidily, let me put it in another way. Not, mind
you, that mistakes have never been made. Sleeping-
draughts—that kind of thing. Even wrong identifi-
cations—that kind of thing. Bricks instead of
bodies. The shockers are full of them. Why, there
was a play produced, only about a month ago, on
that very subject. But, there, let's drop all that. Supposing, Emily, *not* what I said just now. But just
supposing that *he* appeared—*appeared* to have come
back, I mean? This Fiske of ours? What then? Not
him*self*, of course, you know, but. . . . You—you
liked him?"

Emily had drawn back, and had huddled, rather

than seated herself, at the foot of the bed, her hands, like a bird's claws, clutching its edge.

"I see," she replied, though her face at the moment revealed nothing but the mingled glooms and darknesses of doubt and horror. "I *see* you were only persecuting me. You were putting these vile and awful things into my mind, first, merely to watch their effect, and then—and with such gentle fingers! —and then to see the effect of taking them out again. And yet" (she added the words almost pensively, as if a voice had whispered a little secret to her which there was now no immediate need either to explore or to ponder over), "and yet, the cruel memory of them remains to fester. No poor wretch, I suppose, forgets his torturers because they restored him to consciousness: only in order to begin again. Very well, then. Let us be quite, quite clear, and for the last time. . . .

"You ask me if I *liked* him. That question, and you know it, and though I detest saying it, came only out of the old malice and—and cynicism. '*Liked*' him? I liked him beyond words to tell! As one likes —well, being one's self, and being happy. As one likes what has remained true and familiar and of one's very being ever since childhood. Also, I loved him. He was the all, the friend that I had never even dreamed of. Yes, have it all out now! There will be no other chance. Also, I was *in* love with him. Everything that that can imply, body, heart and soul. And you know that, too. And yet. . . . No; you will never, never be able to grasp the true meaning of anything so simple. Not a vestige of that is in your nature. Never. Not at any rate until you break yourself on your own miserable rack. And now, because you had the best of it—and what a best!—you think you can go on and on having the best of me. Taunting me, mocking me, torturing me. Lying and laughing in my face. Who would have believed such lies were even thinkable. Well, now I have owned it. And you can persecute me no more."

"No? 'Quoth the Raven, *Nevermore!*' " A peculiar leer spread over his sallow face. "Ashamed of it?"

" 'Ashamed!' What is there to be ashamed of? What *was* there to be ashamed of? Have you *never* even supposed yourself to be in love? Not even as a child? Before you had the misfortune to meet *me*?"

"Oh, very, very funny!" cried Aubrey, his face wreathed in grimaces. "Misfortune! Misfortune!"— he barked it out so loudly in the room that a thin glass ornament on the dressing-table fairly tinkled with amusement. "But, see here, my pretty romantic bird, what I am saying is—not so much that you *were* in love with the departed gentleman, who, having failed in securing his dot-and-carry-one, *may* have passively accepted his wretched failure and indulged in a sort of go-slow strike against life—but that you still are! Answer me that! And if, living or dead, he came back now. . . . Well, *are* you? Answer me *that*!"

The rasp of his half-suffocated voice seemed to corrode the air. And it appeared as if every contour, every line and edge of her face had altered as he looked at her. Every drop of blood seemed to have withdrawn its last faint red from her cheeks. She had even grown thinner and older, and she was bent almost double, crying.

"Am I? *Am* I? Is that what you ask?"

The sound of her voice was as toneless and drear as some black stagnant pool fringed with muttering rushes in the flats of a marsh where a lost bird is lamenting what never can be uttered or understood. "Well, what if I am? It's not *you* I am concerned with now. Not even *you* can divorce one's very soul from its memories. He is dead. And that—for you— is all that matters."

"All? Indeed, poppet! And yet, supposing, I say, that being dead he yet speaketh?"

Fair, sleek face, rather long and partially hairless smooth head, glossy as dull brass, Aubrey continued to examine the human creature before him as carefully and coldly as if, ardent naturalist, he had brought down a bird of a rare species and was admiring its plumage. Well, it had always been a relief and refreshment to persecute her; even though this time he had gone far nearer the edge, and that irrevocably, than he had intended. Her misery was a kind of dog-like joy to him. And why not? He was being persecuted himself! For jealousy, even if it is concerned with the despised and valueless, can be a bitter draught. Especially if one keeps on secretly sipping at the cup. Especially if. . . . Yes, but— jealousy thrown in or not—would he never, never

know whether or not this 'Mr. Hamilton' of his had,
or had *not*, decided to knock.

"You see, my dear Emily," he went on, "at the
very mention—and, for God's sake, don't keep on
crying, you know how it infuriates me—at the very
mention of his name you let your emotions get the
better of you. There's a word for it—hysteria. It's a
sort of delayed green-sickness—chlorosis. Ask Dr.
McLechlan. I don't blame you; though I am not so
easy a victim myself to such little aberrations. Not
so easy, I say. To be quite truthful. It merely occurred
to me to ask the question. You see, you had already
been brooding, preening your woes. I have lived
with you long enough—oh, how long!—to recognize the aeolian strains. And now a whole year has
gone by; yes, to the very day. Surely that should
have given you time enough to get really and truly
used to things."

The words were little more than sluggishly creep-
ing out of his mouth as though he were talking in
his sleep.

"Don't flatter yourself", he went on, "that I am
seething with any particular emotion. Envy, hatred,
even uncharitableness; that kind of thing. I don't
care a tinker's curse whether you were then, or are
now, in love with him. These women! I don't *care*,
I say. I was never anything more than 'second
thoughts' and then became Enemy No. 1. And yet,
darling, I couldn't have let you go. Now, could I?
Just headlong to your own ruin. Better the sop of
sentimental memories after a year than, well, an

even worse *débâcle*. You have no notion what a
canker a heartsick woman can be. Nor, darling, had
he. And, unfortunate! He left us too early to find
out. So be happy with your treasured woes. Why,
he looks in on you with every mouthful of bread
you eat. He flavours every sip of water. We don't
wear empty faces, sigh at nothing, look over our
shoulder when there is nobody, nothing there—just
for fun. Bless you, no! You can take that from *me*.
. . . But—but, yet again, supposing there had been
love enough? As that pimp of futility ejaculated: 'It
is the cause, my soul; it is the cause.' Did you by any
chance ever read the Plays together—and then 'read
no more'?"

Her face slowly turned in his direction, like a
snail's groping from its shell in search of its way. It
was mottled and distorted with weeping.

"I haven't any notion", she said, "what has happened. What horror. Why you are talking like this;
what—what insanity has come over you. All this
vileness. It is never only what you say, but the in-
sinuations, the poisonous things underneath the
words." A shuddering breath shook her whole body.
"Well, then, listen to me. I know that, while we are
together, I am at your mercy. We are husband and
wife. That was—and that, Heaven help me, still is
and must be—the end of *that*. But you have no
right, before God or man, to question me like this.
Still, here I am, and, as far as I know, in my right
mind, and I will be quite candid with you. If, only
yesterday, he *had* come back, and had wanted me—

are you listening?—then, whether he was living or dead, I should have refused to see him. *Why*, you will ask. Because *then*, I was past bearing it. Ours is ours, his is his, and mine is mine. You merely filthed and made vile the most sacred misfortune the heart can suffer and endure. You dragged it through your mud. For your own poor shifty ends. Ends—though not from my choosing—unattainable now. We had said *our* good-bye, for ever. At least, for any ever known on earth. And now, well . . . I take it back."

"Take *what* back?" shouted Aubrey, as if the contempt and fury now writing on his dead-alive face were also almost past endurance. "Take *what* back? With your rubber water bottles and your furry slippers and your grizzlings and your grousings? Haven't I a right to speak? Haven't I a word to say? Take *what* back?" He had this time—as if under the very blackness of the dry frozen forests—wolfishly yelled the question; and suddenly at sound of it had been seized with a sort of mental rigor. Good God! came the whisper—had his bodiless enemy actually planned and timed his visit for this?

Emily had continued to look at, to watch him; her dark eyes, stupefied with crying, shining out as if from a mask of bone. "That 'for *ever*'," she managed to whisper. "I take *that* back. If now I thought he wanted me, I'd. . . . No," she cried, pushing up her hands to her face, "I cannot bear very much more. I know now that something awful has happened. What is it? Who is it?"

An Anniversary

In the pause that followed, a quiet tapping on the panel of the closed door interrupted them. Aubrey wheeled about as abruptly as an animal that has detected in its nocturnal ravagings the snapping of a withered twig. He turned, and by a few inches gently opened the door.

"What is it?" he said. He was blankly searching the cold impassive face beyond it, sharply lit by the lamps of both bedroom and landing.

"If you please, sir," said Mary, "a Mr. *Hamilton* has called. And, as you told me, I suppose it is 'about a picture'. He stood there; and didn't speak. And after I had inquired—well, I couldn't understand. The mouth moved, but I was not sure if . . . He seemed to have been waiting in the porch. Perhaps he had knocked before, and was listening. But there's of course, the *bell*. And of course, Madam, I shut the door. You never know. . . ."

In spite of her "Madam", her black eyes were fixed on Aubrey's—wide-open and stonily pale-blue —while he tried in vain to keep his lips from trembling. It was as if she had accepted his challenge, even though her attention appeared to be elsewhere. He continued to scrutinize that queer facial chart, this human woman's, which, because of its strength of purpose, because of its honesty and integrity perhaps, he had never been able to decipher. Was this merely a trick? Was this merely a vindictive Mary resenting his pretences? *Was* anyone there? Was it merely some advertising tout? Some ticket-seller? An idiotic coincidence? Had he . . .?

"As a matter of fact," Mary began again, "I had a feeling that he meant he wished to see, not you, sir, but Madam."

A remote yet devilish smile, expressing something between fear, astonishment, hatred, relief and incredulity, was on Aubrey's face as he called back over his shoulder, "Did you hear that, Emily? Someone for *you*. Someone has come for *you*." Then he looked again; but there was no answer.

"Thank you, Mary," he managed to mutter at her, but not quite coherently. "You were perfectly right to shut the door. *That* was no Mr. Hamilton. Some wretched whining tramp, perhaps. He may be gone—by now. If not, say there is illness. No"—he violently shook his head—"don't open. Don't open, I say. No good, now. It is impossible."

He said no more, but slowly shut the door on her, listened for the last rumour of her receding footsteps, and then, with exquisite caution, he carefully turned the key.

He switched off the light, tiptoed to the window and, neatly and punctiliously as a woman, between finger and thumb drew aside the curtain and looked out, and down. Vaguely stirring soundless shadows of trees; shafts of light and of shadow in the small square porch, on the rough red tiles; and nothing besides. Not pausing, even to breathe again, he silently pushed the window ajar, leaned out and looked again. No. . . . He pulled the window to, moistened his lips, pushed the hasp home and drew back the curtains; and this so gently that the metal of curtain-ring scarcely sounded on brass rod. Yet again he listened; then stepped back nimbly; and switched on the light again. What *she* had heard he could not tell. She had fallen sideways along her bed; her face resting between her outstretched arms, as curiously tranquil and composed as if she were already a stranger to all life's longings.

"Holy God!" he muttered.

Then he called, though almost inaudibly, across to her, "Emily! Emily!! . . . What's wrong?"

But no effort could as yet persuade him to go near her. Not for him—not for himself then? But an anniversary! To keep an "assignation"? And Jacob had had to wait *seven* years! How fatuous, how preposterous! Breathing so rapidly that a slight giddiness had swept over consciousness, he paused by her motionless body at as great a distance as the wall admitted stretched out a trembling arm and lifted the telephone receiver from a small and pretty mahogany table that stood, innocent of any share in the proceedings, on the other side of the bed. With extreme deliberation, as if it were an achievement requiring the utmost skill, he dialled a number.

"Is that Dr. Webster's?" he inquired between his lips. . . . "Thank you."

He put his left hand over the mouthpiece and tried to control his breathing.

"Yes. Thank you. This is Mr. Silcot, Mr. Aubrey Silcot. It *is* you, Dr. Webster? Yes, thank you. *Could* you come? . . . Yes, now; at once. I am afraid my wife is seriously ill. Only a fainting fit, perhaps.

Some kind of heart attack. I cannot say. We were talking quite as usual. . . . 'Just home?' I'm sorry. I know what *that* means. But yes; it *is* rather urgent. Yes. . . . Yes—All my thanks! . . ."

He punctiliously returned the receiver to its slumbers, drew back; tiptoed round the bed, and began to listen again.

And in this transfixture, a single commonplace word came sallying nonchalantly up out of his memory as if it were hurt at its not having been duly noticed before—the word "unattainable". Heaven above us! What was *not* unattainable in this world! But *two* victories! A double event! Rage and despair, like a vortex of wind and rain, swept through his mind. The very bridge of his nose seemed to sharpen as presently he stooped over the bed—at a ridiculous corporeal right angle—and his face assumed a stone-like pallor. Slowly, and with the utmost gingerliness, refusing even to touch her pillow, he pushed down his lips close to the ear of his human companion and called softly—a voice cringing yet as ferocious as that of a wolf's in the blackness of snow-bound mountains, and as though he had addressed it into the very centre of outer darkness—cold, callous and illimitable:

"Emily, Emily! Are you there? It's Aubrey. . . I am in a hell of a mess. . . . Hopeless. . . . What did you mean by 'unattainable'?—'un-at-tainable'?"

And again that slowly repeated tapping on the door-panel interrupted him. He crossed the room, and with exquisite caution released the catch in the door, holding this firmly a few inches open.

"What do you want now?" he asked.

"What's going on in there?" said the voice. "Is the doctor coming?"

"The doctor?"

"Yes. . . . And there hasn't been any knock again from that Mr. Hamilton you said was about."

"Oh!" he replied; and was compelled for what seemed yet another infinitesimal yet protracted hole in Eternity to gaze palely back—searching the depths of the motionless cold eyes that were fixed upon his own—before his tongue could utter another word.

BAD COMPANY

It is very seldom that one encounters what would appear to be sheer unadulterated evil in a human face; an evil, I mean, active, deliberate, deadly, dangerous. Folly, heedlessness, vanity, pride, craft, meanness, stupidity—yes. But even Iagos in this world are few, and devilry is as rare as witchcraft.

One winter's evening some little time ago, bound on a visit to a friend in London, I found myself on the platform of one of its many subterranean railway stations. It is an ordeal that one may undergo as seldom as one can. The glare and glitter, the noise, the very air one breathes affect nerves and spirits. One expects vaguely strange meetings in such surroundings. On this occasion, the expectation was justified. The mind is at times more attentive than the eye. Already tired, and troubled with personal cares and problems, which a little wisdom and enterprise should have refused to entertain, I had seated myself on one of the low, wooden benches to the left of the entrance to the platform, when, for no conscious reason, I was prompted to turn my head in the direction of a fellow traveller, seated across the gangway on the fellow to my bench some few yards away.

What was wrong with him? He was enveloped in a loose cape or cloak, sombre and motionless. He appeared to be wholly unaware of my abrupt scrutiny. And yet I doubt it; for the next moment, although the door of the nearest coach gaped immediately opposite him, he had shuffled into the compartment I had entered myself, and now in its corner, confronted me, all but knee to knee. I could have touched him with my hand. We had, too, come at once into an even more intimate contact than that of touch. Our eyes—his own fixed in a dwelling and lethargic stare—had instantly met, and no less rapidly mine had uncharitably recoiled, not only in misgiving, but in something little short of disgust. The effect resembled that of an acid on milk, and for the time being cast my thoughts into confusion. Yet that one glance had taken him in.

He was old—over seventy. A wide-brimmed rusty and dusty black hat concealed his head—a head fringed with wisps of hair, lank and paper-grey. His loose, jaded cheeks were of the colour of putty; the thin lips above the wide unshaven and dimpled chin showing scarcely a trace of red. The cloak suspended from his shoulders mantled him to his shins. One knuckled, cadaverous, mittened hand clasped a thick ash stick, its handle black and polished with long usage. The only sign of life in his countenance was secreted in his eyes—fixed on mine—hazed and dully glistening, as a snail in winter is fixed to a wall. There was a dull deliberate challenge in them, and, as I fancied, something more than that. They suggested that he had been in wait for me; that for him, it was almost "well met!".

For minutes together I endeavoured to accept their challenge, to make sure. Yet I realized, fascinated the while, that he was well aware of the futility of this attempt, as a snake is of the restless, fated bird in the branches above its head.

Such a statement, I am aware, must appear wildly exaggerated, but I can only record my impression. It was already lateish—much later than I had intended. The passengers came and went, and, whether intentionally or not, none consented to occupy the seat vacant beside him. I fixed my eyes on an advertisement—that of a Friendly Society I remember!—immediately above his head, with the intention of watching him in the field of an eye that I could not persuade to meet his own in full focus again.

He had instantly detected this ingenuous device. By a fraction of an inch he had shifted his grasp upon his stick. So intolerable, at length, became the physical—and psychical—effect of his presence on me that I determined to leave the train at the next station, and there to await the next. And at this precise moment, I was conscious that he had not only withdrawn his eyes but closed them.

I was not so easily to free myself of his company. A glance over my shoulder as, after leaving the train, I turned towards the lift, showed him hastily groping his way out of the carriage. The metal gate clanged. The lift slid upwards and, such is the con-

trariness of human nature, a faint disappointment
followed. One may, for example, be appalled and
yet engrossed in reading an account of some act of
infamous cruelty.

Concealing myself as best I could at the book-
stall, I awaited the next lift-load. Its few passengers
having dispersed, he himself followed. In spite of
age and infirmity, he *had*, then, ascended alone the
spiral staircase. Glancing, it appeared, neither to
right nor left, he passed rapidly through the barrier.
And yet—*had* he not seen me?

The ticket collector raised his head, opened his
mouth, watched his retreating figure, but made no
attempt to retrieve *his*. It was dark now—the dark of
London. In my absence underground, minute frozen
pellets of snow had fallen, whitening the streets and
lulling the sound of the traffic. On emerging into the
street, he turned in the direction of the next station
—my own. Yet again—had he, or had he not, been
aware that he was being watched? However that
might be, my journey lay his way, and that way my
feet directed me; although I was already later than I
had intended. I followed him, led on no doubt in
part— merely by the effect he had had on me. Some
twenty or thirty yards ahead, his dark shapelessness
showed—distinct against the whitening pavement.

The waters of the Thames, I was aware, lay on my
left. A muffled blast from the siren of a tug announced its presence. Keeping my distance, I followed him on. One lamp-post—two—three. At
that, he seemed to pause for a moment, as if to

listen, momentarily glanced back (as I fancied) and vanished.

When I came up with it, I found that this third lamp-post vaguely illuminated the mouth of a narrow, lightless alley between highish walls. It led me, after a while, into another alley, yet dingier. The wall on the left of this was evidently that of a large garden; on the right came a row of nondescript houses, looming up in their neglect against a starless sky.

The first of these houses *appeared* to be occupied. The next two were vacant. Dingy curtains, soot-grey against their snowy window-sills, hung over the next. A litter of paper and refuse—abandoned by the last long gust of wind that must have come whistling round the nearer angle of the house—lay under the broken flight of steps up to a mid-Victorian porch. The small snow clinging to the bricks and to the worn and weathered cement of the wall only added to its gaunt lifelessness.

In the faint hope of other company coming my way, and vowing that I would follow no further than to the outlet of yet another pitch-black and uninviting alley or court—which might indeed prove a dead end—I turned into it. It was then that I observed, in the rays of the lamp over my head, that in spite of the fineness of the snow and the brief time that had elapsed, there seemed to be no trace on its surface of recent footsteps.

A faintly thudding echo accompanied me on my way. I have found it very useful—in the country—

always to carry a small electric torch in my great-coat pocket; but for the time being I refrained from using it. This alley proved not to be blind. Beyond a patch of waste ground, a nebulous, leaden-grey vacancy marked a loop here of the Thames—I decided to go no further; and then perceived a garden gate in the wall to my right. It was ajar, but could not long have been so because no more than an instant's flash of my torch showed marks in the snow of its recent shifting. And yet there was little wind. On the other hand, here was the open river; just a breath of a breeze across its surface might account for this. The cracked and blistered paint was shimmering with a thin coat of rime—of hoar-frost, and as if a finger had but just now scrawled it there, a clumsy arrow showed, its "V" pointing inward. A tramp, an errand-boy, mere accident might have accounted for this. It may indeed have been a mark made some time before on the paint.

I paused in an absurd debate with myself, chiefly I think because I felt some little alarm at the thought of what might follow; yet led on also by the conviction that I had been intended, decoyed to follow. I pushed the gate a little wider open, peered in, and made my way up a woody path beneath ragged un-pruned and leafless fruit trees towards the house. The snow's own light revealed a ramshackle flight of steps up to a poor, frenchified sort of canopy above french windows, one-half of their glazed doors ajar. I ascended, and peered into the intense gloom beyond it. And thus and then prepared to retrace my steps as quickly as possible, I called (in tones as near those of a London policeman as I could manage):

"Hello there! Is anything wrong? Is anyone wanted?" After all, I could at least explain to my fellow-passenger if he appeared that I found both his gate and his window open; and the house was hardly pleasantly situated.

No answer was returned to me. In doubt and disquietude, but with a conviction that all was not well, I flashed my torch over the walls and furniture of the room and its heavily framed pictures. How could anything be "well"—with unseen company such as this besieging one's senses! Ease and pleasant companionship, the room may once have been capable of giving; in its dirt, cold, and neglect it showed nothing of that now. I crossed it, paused again in the passage beyond it, and listened. I then entered the room beyond that. Venetian blinds, many of the slats of which had outworn their webbing, and heavy, crimson chenille side-curtains concealed its windows.

The ashes of a fire showed beyond rusty bars of the grate under a black marble mantelpiece. An oil lamp on the table, with a green shade, exuded a stink of paraffin; beyond was a table littered with books and papers, and an overturned chair. There I could see the bent-up old legs, perceptibly lean beneath the trousers, of the occupant of the room. In no doubt of whose remains these were, I drew near, and with bared teeth and icy, trembling fingers, drew back the fold of the cloak that lay over the face. Death has a strange sorcery. A shuddering revulsion of feeling took possession of me. This cold, once genteel, hideous, malignant room—and this!

The skin of the blue loose cheek was drawn tight over the bone; the mouth lay a little open, showing the dislodged false teeth beneath; the dull unspeculative eyes stared out from beneath lowered lids towards the black mouth of the chimney above the fireplace. Vileness and iniquity had left their marks on the lifeless features, and yet it was rather with compassion than with horror and disgust that I stood regarding them. What desolate solitude, what misery must this old man, abandoned to himself, have experienced during the last years of his life; encountering nothing but enmity and the apprehension of his fellow creatures. I am not intending to excuse or even commiserate what I cannot understand, but the almost complete absence of any goodness in the human spirit, cannot but condemn the heart to an appalling isolation. Had he been murdered, or had he come to a violent but natural end? In either case, horror and terror must have supervened.

That I had been enticed, deliberately led on, to this discovery I hadn't the least doubt, extravagant though this, too, may seem. Why? What for?

I could not bring myself to attempt to light the lamp. Besides, in that last vigil, it must have burnt itself out. My torch revealed a stub of candle on the mantelpiece. I lit that. He seemed to have been engaged in writing when the enemy of us all had approached him in silence and had struck him down.

Bad Company

A long and unsealed envelope lay on the table. I drew out the contents—a letter and a Will, which had been witnessed some few weeks before, apparently by a tradesman's boy and, possibly, by some derelict charwoman, Eliza Hinks. I knew enough about such things to be sure that the Will was valid and complete. This old man had been evidently more than fairly rich in this world's goods, and reluctant to surrender them. The letter was addressed to his two sisters: "To my two Sisters, Amelia and Maude." Standing there in the cold and the silence, and utterly alone—for, if any occupant of the other world had decoyed me there, there was not the faintest hint in consciousness that he or his influence was any longer present with me—I read the vilest letter that has ever come my way. Even in print. It stated that he knew the circumstances of these two remaining relatives—that he was well aware of their poverty and physical conditions. One of them, it seemed, was afflicted with Cancer. He then proceeded to explain that, although they should by the intention of their mother have had a due share in her property and in the money she had left, it rejoiced him to think that his withholding of this knowledge must continually have added to their wretchedness. Why he so hated them was only vaguely suggested.

The Will he had enclosed with the letter left all that he died possessed of to—of all human establishments that need it least—the authorities of Scotland Yard. It was to be devoted, it ran, to the detection of such evil-doers as are ignorant or imbecile enough to leave their misdemeanours and crimes detectable.

It is said that confession is good for the soul. Well then, as publicly as possible, I take this opportunity of announcing that, there and then, I made a little heap of envelope, letter and Will on the hearth and put a match to them. When every vestige of the paper had been consumed, I stamped the ashes down. I had touched nothing else. I would leave the vile, jaded, forsaken house to reveal its own secret; and I might ensure that that would not be long delayed.

What continues to perplex me is that so far as I can see no other agency but that of this evil old recluse himself had led me to my discovery. Why? Can it have been with this very intention? I stooped down and peeped and peered narrowly in under the lowered lids in the light of my torch, but not the feeblest flicker, remotest signal—or faintest syllabling echo of any message rewarded me. Dead fish are less unseemly.

And yet. Well—we are all of us, I suppose, at any extreme *capable* of remorse and not utterly shut against repentance. Is it possible that this priceless blessing is not denied us even when all that's earthly else appear to have come to an end?

A BEGINNING

"In a word, a man were better relate himself, to a Statua, or picture, than to suffer
his thoughts to pass in smother."
                    BACON: *Essay on Friendship*

In a corner of the Count's old writing desk I
found the Diary and Letters which follow. For
the sake of brevity one or two passages have been
omitted; otherwise, the young man speaks for himself; a task, apparently, by no means uncongenial.
Let his youth be his apology. The letters are here,
just as they were found, in a bundle wrapped up in
brown paper, tied with a piece of red tape; and
simply marked on the cover with a big F.

April 25th 18—. In very low spirits all day. It seems
to me that one's moods keep up a kind of see-saw;
so that the slightest thing swoops one mid-air, or
plunges one into Hades. This is weak. Perhaps Fanny
does not quite understand me. She does not *come out*
to me. I sometimes wonder if I should not have done
something really great in the world, if I had had

someone who passionately believed in me, a companion for my higher self. But after all, obscurity is more philosophical—and certainly less troublesome! Yet I do detest mere flippant tittle-tattle. Anything abstract depresses women. At least so I find it. I am sick to death of my miserable self. All the virtue is gone out of this musty stolid world. *Væ Victis!*

April 26th. Met Fanny this afternoon in the High Street. She was out shopping, so I walked a little way with her. But I did not intend to humble myself, craving forgiveness for what I had not done, or intended to do; and she kept looking at everyone, and answering vacantly, and her face was all indifferent. So I asked her to tell me what I had done. Whereupon, of course, she began to cry—in a corner by a bonnet shop. . . I could not help being in a rage, because some counter-jumper was watching us from between the bonnets. And then she flared up, and told me to go away for ever, because she hated me to see her crying! So I shook hands and told her about the counter-jumper.

"That's just it," she said, "you simply glory in making me look silly. I know I *am* silly, but it's not so very clever to bring me here to be laughed at by people." Of course all this was quite unreasonable, and I pointed it out to her. But we made it up afterwards, and went into Martellini's and had some tea. I don't understand women; and yet I do if I think them out. They don't understand themselves; *that's* pretty certain.

A Beginning

April 26th. (Letter from Fanny to Nicholas.)

10.15 *p.m.*
My bedroom.

My dear Nicholas,

Mama *did* see us in the pastrycook's; and is extremely vexed. She says it looks so *vulgar*. I wonder if she thought as much about looks in papa's days! But we must not do it again, though I did enjoy myself very much indeed, dear. We are going to a Concert to-night—second row; will you come and sit somewhere else, and come up *accidentally* afterwards, because I haven't another ticket? Mamma and Laura are coming, and I dare say Mr. Herriot will be there; so that will be alright. *I* think he cringes, but Laura says it's policy. I hate policy if one's feelings tell one not, don't you? I'm sorry for being cross, dear, but sometimes you seem as if you were cold almost on purpose. Do please come to the concert and sit where I can see you. I shall not enjoy it the least bit if you don't. Mrs. Bolsover is going to sing "The May Queen" ! ! ! and Harriet, the guitar in the second part.

From ever your affectionate,

FANNY.

P.S. Do you think that impudent shopman *really* saw us?

April 27th. Letter from Uncle R. Threatens to mew me up in Cornwall if I laze about here. There are two sides to that question, sweet guardian! Last night I dreamed vividly of the old house. I have not seen it for thirteen years. I was looking in by the iron gates and saw Mother in a shawl walking in the garden. And there was a fire burning in the dining room, the flames were shining in the window. And then, just as Mother looked up, the dream went out —as if Morpheus had taken the light away. There is a tinge of melancholy in old things. I feel as if I were a traitor in having quite forgotten it all. I shall go down one afternoon and revive the dead past. My memory seems haunted now. Of course this is non-sense, and it is just thought-connection. Letter from Fanny. So Madam *did* espy us over our banquet. She puts me in mind of a gooseberry that has spent all its sweetness on its size. Some men have no vocation to be a husband. The intellectual life is highest. Well, I suppose I shall be a maudlin old greybeard in time. We all come to it if we are such fools as to live long enough. New coat and trousers came home; shall send latter back to-morrow; very bad fit.

> *Fanny, I gently muse of thee*
> *In midnight Solitude,*
> *The memory of thy melting orb*
> *Is like a beatitude.*

> *And oft the breezes waft thy name*
> *Unto my wakeful sense;*
> *Thy loving heart were all my Fame*
> *And all my recompence.*

To bed!

A Beginning

April 28th. Warm. Sent clothes back. Nil.

April 29th. The Scarlet Lady! ! ! I started off about 2 o.c. And there, as if all these years it had been preserved under a glass case, was the old place. I dawdled slowly up the narrow street. There in the sawdust sprawled the same narrow curly retriever dog (or a grandson); there in "gilty" row stood the same shabby dusty books in the "Library", and there the same old Mrs. Perks (now in the apple-dumpling stage, with silvering hair) peering between the illuminated texts. But everything seemed so curiously *small*. I seemed to myself a kind of Werther, or for that matter, a Rip Van Winkle. Not a soul recognized me. But I enjoyed the secrecy of the thing. On I went, and at the hilltop under the chestnut trees burst out upon the heath. And like the effeminate ass I am, I had to blink to keep from crying.

Well, I am not ashamed of it, if it was so. If a thing is, it is. And if that is one's philosophy in life, one is safe from the sham senseless mob. On again I went between the gorse bushes. And about five in the afternoon came in sight of the house. There it was, just as I remembered it. I went on slowly. "Hame, hame, hame, hame!" I took hold of the bars of the gate and stared in at the familiar place. There were red curtains in the dining room windows; smoke was winding up from the chimney, and an old man was digging in the kitchen garden; I could just see him over the hedge. And while I was standing there, staring like an owl, I heard the *cessation* of footsteps.

A Beginning

(It's a very curious example of the senses being disconnected with the Ego, because I am quite convinced I had not actually heard the footsteps themselves.)

I turned round, and there stood a girl, top to toe in scarlet. She stood there, rather slim and pale, looking out gravely at me from under her beaver hat. I can't for the life of me think who she reminded me of. At last I managed to stutter out some apology, and opened the gate for her. She bowed solemnly and, still looking at me with her bright grave eyes, passed through. The gate swung to after her, and up to the heavens went its old whinnying squeal. And just as I was about to go, she turned towards me with one hand held irresolutely out of her muff, the red sleeve hanging down like the wing of a wounded bird. She frowned a little, raising and lowering her eyebrows (a little trick of hers) and to my intense surprise, spoke to me. Her voice was soft and quick with a lot of notes in it, rather pretty.

"Pray forgive me," she said very nervously, "but perhaps, I—are you—perhaps you would like to walk in the garden?"

Consequently, I must needs out with why I was staring in at her gate. Anyone would think that I had never set eyes on a woman before. Still she *was* rather disconcerting. "O, then, pray come in!" she said. "My father would be so very pleased to have you see it all again. I think, you know—it's very strange —but even when I saw you standing here at the gate as I came up, I recognized you; the stoop, the turn of the head—just a little something in the attitude. But, dear me, how ridiculous this must seem to you. For you have never so much as seen the glimmer of the ghost of me—have you? Dreaming or waking. I wonder. But I know *you*, and very well too; though it is not quite the same face—wiser, you know; no, not wiser—more experienced. It's a very long time ago since you lived here."

She might have been talking to herself; her voice ran on so easily. "Thirteen years," I said. "But how——"

"Yes, so it is, so it is," she answered, exactly thirteen years—thirteen! . . . My father bought the house, you know."

"Then he must have bought it from my—from the executors."

"Yes, poor mite; and you not so high then; just up to my waist here, I should think. And long straight hair, and big eyes in a wan face. Oh, I have pitied you sometimes." I am not sure that I was overgrateful for her pity. She laughed mysteriously, and knocked at the door. A middle-aged woman in slippers opened to her. She looked quickly at me with pale grey eyes. "This is Nicholas, Helen," said the Scarlet Lady, and looked back at me again.

"Is that so, Miss?" said the woman. She smoothed her sleek hair with the palm of her hand. An abominable person!

"There, you see! 'Miss' added to me. I know your name too. You must come in and see my father. And we'll have tea, please, Helen; Mr. Nicholas must taste my honey. The garden, I am afraid, is not nearly so prim and proper as it should be—all waste and sweetness. Thomas is growing old, and the birds come in legions, so of course the fruit is theirs, cherries and strawberries! We haven't had a dishful for years. But then they sing—the birds, you know —just as you too must have heard them thirteen years ago." She rambled on without stopping, as if she had known me all her life; and yet I am sure she was nervous of me because her hands were trembling. She had opened the door of my mother's little parlour. And instantly a picture flashed in on me of the little room in the old days, with its muslin curtains and its carpet of moss-roses, and its blue silk work-basket, and my mother's little favourite cane-chair, where she used to sit in the bow-window over her needlework.

But now instead here a gaunt old gentleman sat bolt upright in a stiff wooden chair before an empty grate. Rows of musty folios to duodecimos lined the shelves in the walls; and there was a lame old clock ticking. On one side of the bow-window stood a mouldering bureau, gaping and choke-full of papers. It reeked of mortality. The old boy had reluctantly put down his book and now got up stiffly from his chair when we approached him—a lamp-post of a man, with a large high nose. He bowed absent-eyedly over my hand like a schoolmaster; until I felt I was being carpeted. And on bare boards too!

"This gentleman has come to look over the house and walk in the garden, Father," said Florence. He bowed again. Florence moved her eyebrows up and down, and coughed—another little trick of hers.

"It is really *his* house, of course, and we are just barbarians—interlopers. He was the little boy, who came into the world here and who knows every nook and cranny, every cupboard—*corner* too, I'll be bound, and the views spread out from every window. Like a picture-book. He says *Sesame*, and there it is. I found him peeping through the bars of the gate just as he used to peep—ten inches high. So what could I do but behave unladylike-ly, and ask him to come in." She went to the window, squeezing in between the bureau and the panels of the wall and turned her back on us, standing quite still. It was curious to see her scarlet in the bare room. The old fellow's face was like a mask.

"I shall be happy to be of any service to you, sir," he said. "The roots of childhood strike very deep. In the first years we learn our whereabouts. I have no doubt the house recalls much to your remembrance. Will you please be quite at liberty here; I think I once had the honour of meeting your mother many . . ."

" 'Mother'! His mother?" said the girl whipping round. "And this is the first. . . . Oh, tell me. . . . Oh but. . . ." She eyed me anxiously as if she feared she might have hurt me. "Now you must come and see the garden," she added, breaking off with a smile, "or else night will be catching us up. Will you?"

"Pray excuse me, sir, if I do not accompany you into the garden," said the old gentleman. "It is, I fear, but poorly tended. Things are left to grow in their own free way. My daughter prefers it so; and I think I prefer it so too. Please put yourself quite at your ease, and spare us nothing to be of service to you." I saw Florence squeeze his hand as she passed.

"Isn't it splendid?" she said. "I always told you he'd come——"

"Fancies, fancies, my dear child," said the old fellow vacantly. "It is hazardous to put your faith in fancies. Everything passes. Things are what they are in essence; there is no change."

He said this or some such stuff, standing erect, as if he were some antique philosopher with the gods for audience. And then for the first time I noticed he was a clergyman. A remarkable old man. However eccentric. *Real.*

"And now I suppose I must tell you the secret," said Florence, as she led me out and bade me wait at the foot of the staircase, while she ran up, singing. And that gave me time to think.

It seemed awfully strange to find myself standing alone in the house again, so acutely familiar, and yet utterly changed. And it was devilish melancholy. I seemed to hear again my mother's footstep behind me; and when the strange woman—strange to *me*—came upstairs from the kitchen I fancied for a moment it was her maid, Martha, who used always to be muttering about the house with her feather broom.

Eheu! I have gone through many years and a good deal of experience since those days. And I see life in its true colours. I suppose it's rather ridiculous to be writing down all this stuff. Still, it seemed even in its own time a kind of epoch or crisis in my life. Besides, this girl was quite different from all my previous experience of her monotonous sex—so whimsical and mysterious, and almost dictatorial to me. Nor was she a bit pretty, or even beautiful—except her eyes. But after all, in the words of the proverb, beauty is only skin deep. "*The Lady in Scarlet,*" *a Romance in three volumes by a new, original and talented Author ! ! !*

When she came downstairs she had taken off her hat, and her dark hair was drawn back loosely from her forehead, quite plain. There's a sort of curve about her eyes: it's difficult to describe, but her face is so much herself; not the least bit like Fanny.

"Now, come into the garden," she said, "and I'll show it thee." I remember the "thee" distinctly! So out I went after her into the garden. In an instant I shrunk up into the breeches Age. There it was quite unchanged, only a little wilder and greener; cherry and apple and hawthorn, lilac and laburnum; and melting sweet with wallflowers—it was Mother. All herself.

"There, Mr. Nicholas," she said brightly, leaning forward an instant, "have we been fickle? Do you remember?" And then her face was all grave again. "How am I to excuse myself," she continued, "I am ashamed to think of it. Up at the window there, looking out over the tree-tops, I saw it all in a flash. And I was utterly ashamed. I don't know what you must think of me, but whatever it is, it is true; still, if you have the heart of the little boy whose face I know so well, you will easily forgive me. For, don't you see, living here alone day by day, and day by day, one learns to conduct one's self as if one were only and always in one's own company. With other people of course you must be in their company, and . . . there, think it in your own words. At any rate. . . . Well?"

I mumbled that it was very kind of her and all that, and that "I was much obliged to Mr. . . ."

"Our name is Lindsay," she broke in quickly. "I forgot. My father has no curacy or anything of that kind here. We just live on together. . . ."

"He is very fortunate to have such a companion," I said, and nearly bit my tongue off. I can't help saying silly things to women. Her frown went away, she closed her lips, and looked almost distressed. She shook herself, and all the ring had gone out of her voice.

"Well, as I was coming downstairs, that was not in the least what I wanted to say. Yet somehow or other I have to explain myself, and this is the only way. This picture. I don't want now to show it you in the least; not now. But after we had moved into the house, we found a litter of old papers in one of my father's cupboards. And this was among them. I stole it. I hate showing it to you—it is like betraying a friend. But still I must do so, and please if you wouldn't mind, will you give it me back quickly?"

After all this beating about the bush she put into my hand a little pencil drawing of a child framed in

an oval of ebony. And underneath it was written in
my old infantile scrawl, "This is me, Nicholas." Of
course I remembered it instantly. It was the little
drawing Mother made of me years ago. I remember
her standing me by the copper coal-scuttle in her
little parlour, and afterwards sitting me on her knee
and telling me what to write and guiding my hand.
I can almost feel the heat of the fire on my bare legs,
and my tongue anxiously protruded while I
scrawled. I told her that it was my mother's drawing. "She used to play with me sometimes," I said.

"Poor mite," she said, smiling in her old way.
"And have you been happy since? Oh, what a fool
I am to be asking such questions. Well, anyhow,
now you know why I—liked to see you—and it
accounts for my pitiful familiarity—my ignorance
—does it?"

I stumbled over some remark, repeating, "kindness, pleasure", and so on.

"Ah," she said, and took the picture from me.
"Dreams! Other people are not like me—and there's
no conceit in that! I cannot talk to you, Mr. Nicholas; you're listening with all your manners on. And
I have forgotten the few I ever had. Well; we must
go in." She hesitated in the porch, half smiling, yet
frowning. "Have you ever said to yourself when
anything vividly happens—or you see anything
sharply——" She jerked her hand towards the garden. "*This* I shall remember *always*; just as it is. And
when the remembrance comes—well, it isn't quite
what one expected. Come in, Mr. Nicholas; I don't

know, and will never ask your surname. 'This is you, Nicholas'; that is all."

We took tea in what, I suppose, is the drawing-room (our dining room) very old fashioned and rather shabby. All the house is drab and silent. Mr. L. sat in an old leather armchair, his knees at an acute angle. And ever and again, his eyes would melt out of reverie, and he would make a remark. He seemed to be at pains to be good company, and to be always forgetting his good intentions. He munched, like an old mare, and sipped five cups of tea, and his nose was beaked between his eyes. So on the whole I felt devilish *de trop*. It was a mutes' tea-party for me. Florence hardly spoke at all. She seemed to have been exhausted with talking, although her eyes were still smouldering. So we stolidly sat on, with an occasional supping noise from Mr. Lindsay, and the whistling of the birds in the garden. By and by, to my intense relief, Mr. L. put down his cup for the last time, and sat with his hands on his knees.

"I doubt, sir," he said presently, as if my very thoughts had been audible, "I doubt if this house was ever so quiet in your childhood. We are hermits. And solitude attenuates the rumour of the world. But I hope you will pay us another visit some day. We do not order ourselves much by formality, as you perceive, but you will be welcome." It was evidently a hint for me to be gone; and I jumped at the opportunity. So I thanked him again for his courtesy, and shook him by the hand. He stood up stiff as a lamp-post and seemed to gaze down out of his vacant blue eyes like a caged bird.

Florence showed me to the door. "There", she said as she opened it, "it is growing dusk. I am afraid we have detained you. Have I?"

"*Really*, no," I said, "I cannot tell you how grateful I am. Fancy to have come to an *empty* house, or to have found it all——" "Well, it would not have been faithless," she said, "it would never have been that. We love its silence and solitude; or rather we do not feel them. We are egoists. Our fancies bewitch our eyes. . . . That is *my* garden," she looked far away over the dusky heath, dark and boundless to the shining of the stars. "And will you come again, do you think? Dear me, how hard it is to get used to all the conventions. Good-bye, Mr. Nicholas. And I shall keep your picture, and—unless you do come again with your real self on your arm—shall forget you. How still the night is! It is almost as if someone were listening. . . ."

Here endeth the first chapter. And once again I am in my own sweet company, thank Jupiter.

It's the dolefullest household I ever was in. She had no genuine interest in me, I think. She scarcely gave me an opportunity to speak; she harped so incessantly on the drawing—rather childish, I thought. But so is she, with not a symptom of *savoir faire*. Yet her face is old. She must be at least nineteen or so. I could read that face like a book one moment, and then she frowned or something, and I was all wrong.

Her faintest smile changes it; now and then it is almost as if she were beautiful. I was miserably awkward in her company, not at all myself. She must think me absurdly green. There's some skeleton in the old father's cupboard, I'll wager. A broken love affair, perhaps. Anyhow, I loathe tea-parties. Why can't people speak out as God made them?

As I look back I realize that she did not even shake hands with me—seemed almost to avoid doing so. I shouldn't think she really takes the slightest interest in me; she's an Egoist. And here I am, wasting all this time (not to mention weeks of diary-space) scribbling rubbish. I shall give up trying to analyse every little thing I do or think. I don't suppose Shakespeare or Napoleon did. The real thing is to forget one's self and live for others. How much wiser is a man than his tongue!—Wrote to Uncle Robert. Marvellously starry night.

April 29th. Went to concert with "Madame" and Fanny. Madame is good-humoured enough, but otherwise a more or less meaningless mixture of frivolity, sententiousness and Scandal. It seemed as if I had not seen F. for weeks. I said nothing about my visit.
April 30th. Dreamed again of the old house. It was sunny, and the door opened, and old L. came out into the garden—half encircled in a nimbus!! Henceforward I shall keep an account of my dreams, I think. Man dreams probably all the time he is asleep; because *thinking* is to *be*, and we can't become

nothing, or we should remain so. Took a constitutional in the afternoon, met G. M. A little Frenchiness is a dangerous thing. Mrs. Giles interred at 3.30.

May 1st. May-day. Awoke with, and in, a fit of the miserables. Wet. Read some of that affected minx, Addison. He has no more essential knowledge of human nature than a fly! Have a good mind to write and thank F. L. for my visit. They were very civil, considering. Young, young man, Beware!

May 3rd. Learn to control thy thoughts lest thy thoughts learn to control thee!

May 6th. Went for a walk with Fanny. She never once ceased chattering about her sister's forthcoming wedding; a heathen custom; and we brag about our civilization, forsooth! It's no better than any other primitive rite, and so are Funerals. Bury me in an apple-barrel at the cross-roads! say I. It's more real and human, at any rate, than crapulous coachmen and crocodile tears. Fanny asked me why I was "different". She does not understand that a man may have more than one side to his character and nature. I am not a machine, although I may some day be a husband.

May 5th. Went down again this morning. It seemed as if the caravans of Spring were camping on the heath. There was a kind of immense warm stillness, a haze of sunshine—and all dazzlingly green. And almost the first person I encountered was F. L. herself.

She was sitting on a little knoll of turf, her face turned away from me. And though all her finery was gone, yet I recognized her instantly. I

walked quickly over the turf, but though I scarcely
made a sound she heard me and turned quickly. By
the brightness of her eyes I fancied for a moment she
had been crying. But I think she looks best in black.
All women do. She put out her hand, looking at me;
and something in the gesture, or in her expression,
reminded me strangely of Mother. I made some silly
remark about it's not being a *red*-letter day.

"Don't talk about *me*," she said, "I am dead-alive,
dulled out, fey. And the scarlet—I think I wore it
out of spite. I said to myself, I will be April, too.
And indeed I was—the First! . . . I thought you might
come again *before* to-day. I always believe people
will do what I hope they will—until they don't. But
there, do not listen. 'The rain is over and gone.' "
She clasped her hands like a child, "I often think . . . ",
she began again, almost as if she were speaking to
herself; and then it was just as if a shadow had come
over her face.

"What do you often think?" I said.

"Never mind," she said under her breath; then
she looked up at me with one of her curious smiles.
"Will you come back with me? Father would be
delighted to see you. Will you come? Besides, I have
not showed you half the house yet. Come, and you
shall go straight back, and be a child again. And to
tell you the truth I want to get used to the idea of
you—grown-up, and polite, and clever and all that.
Oh, you are sadly altered. Still I want to see you as
you are, and fit you into the house. Will you come?"

I could not be boor enough to refuse, though it

was a precious nuisance. She was different from last time. Beneath all she said was something else; I can't express it exactly. But I was not the least bit more at my ease with her.

Mr. Lindsay rose up lank and stark as ever. Poor old man, his face does not practise his philosophical sermons. He sat there, his white cravat awry, a jagged frown on his forehead. Time has dried him up and ploughed him deep. Still he's frightfully heavy, and for the life of me I couldn't see the point of most of what he said. He seems to speak by rote. Gad, let me die green! I saw the woman, Helen; I suppose she's a kind of housekeeper.

She brought Florence a wrap, and wound it round and round her as if she was bent on embalming her. I wanted to say "good afternoon" to her, just to be civil; but she didn't give me a chance. So F. and I walked up and down in the garden together. "You see", she said, "everything is the same, and time is a myth. I need not think unless I please, need I?" She's always saying peculiar things like that. I shan't write it all down, but I can remember. She asked me all about myself. She leans forward with her questions. I have never met anybody with so many mannerisms. But I did not mention much. I told her about when I was at school, and all I remembered about my mother. And yet I hate talking about myself; like the hypocrite I am. And I have promised to go again.

May 9th. 9 p.m. Showery. Feel but poorly. Had rather a bad night. Fanny was in a pet this evening;

and I too. I was never intended for a married life. I loathe being gloated over as if I were a fatted calf for the wedding feast. And 'pon my oath, I'm not after "Madam's" spoons, nor Madam's chastity neither! Wrote to Fanny. Bill from Paige; moderate.

(Letter from Fanny to Nicholas, dated May 6th)

My own dear, dear Nick,

You did not mean to hurt my feelings, and I was just as bad, and worse. Mama asked me why my eyes were so red; but I managed to put her off. I suppose I *am* rather fanciful, dear, but indeed you did not seem quite the same towards me, and I can't help fancies coming, because I am not very pretty and attractive I know. But I won't in the future. I have sent you the Smoking Cap, I hope it won't be crumpled. Will you wear it for my sake, I worked it all myself in my room, except of course the design. The top of the N is not quite right, but it's not nice stuff to work on, and just now there are so many things to do I hardly know which way to turn. Papa said last night you had a good head on your shoulders, it doesn't sound much, but from him it means a good deal. Practicalness is not everything, whatever Mama may say. Are you quite sure you are not in the least bit cross with me now. I will try to understand, if you will be patient, because I get so confused. Goodnight, dear, I feel rather mournful tonight. I don't know what I should do without you.

From ever your affectionate

FANNY.

A Beginning

P.S. It's quite untrue about G. M. but I thought you did not care, and that made me angry and hateful.

May 8th. Sick headache. Fanny staying at her aunt's for a day or two.

May 9th. Met F. on heath. She compelled me to run a race with her; we were like two children, and then, as I warned her, she had a fit of coughing and grew deadly white. She's not very strong I fancy. So I made her take my arm, and she was very quiet all the way home. Only when I'm there I forget the shackles of conventionality, and am my real self. She is very difficult to understand—all index and chapter headings. But I am sure she does not do it on purpose, because she is very sincere. I think it's rather morbid. There is something unnatural in a woman intentionally *thinking* much. A woman's thoughts are almost always instinct, and we should not overstep Nature's limitations. Why, love itself is absolutely unreasonable. You can't prove it because then it simply goes.

May 10th. Fanny returned home. Mrs. Mann thinks my voice is tenor in quality. Wants me to join her singing Academy. Discontented.

May 11th. F. Took tea in the garden under the Apple trees. But it began to be misty towards evening, and the old gentleman insisted on F. going into the house. But I don't think she wanted to. She showed me her books. There is a long dark painting of the Madonna above the mantelpiece. She does not draw or paint or do fancy needlework or anything of that kind. "I could if I had not tried," she said laughing, when I asked her. And that's rather good, because it's just as I feel about some things. I almost think I like the quiet of the house, and the heath stretching out far away. Generally F. is very restless, but tonight she seemed scarcely to breathe, and though it sounds very absurd, you almost see her thoughts in her face; her eyes especially. Sometimes I catch Mr. L's eyes fixed on me in a clear vacant stare, as if they had carried a message to his brains and were awaiting a reply. I don't fancy he likes me. F. says he suffers a good deal of pain; from some internal complaint, I suppose. Of course it's a pithy thing to ignore pain, but after all it's only bragging to one's self. It's not philosophical to be excessive, but to take things as they come, and not to put on airs in private. I grow more and more melancholy every day.

May 12th. Spent the evening at Millar's. Fanny there and a Miss Gwynn—fair hair and thin. A languishing ninny. She told F. I had the air of a flirt, silly chit. Rather good fun to talk to, though. Fancied Fanny was not in very good spirits. I can't be forever at her heels. . . . Voices in the air, as if someone were calling; I looked out and there was a crescent moon among the stars. It's a mysterious world.

May 13th. O how I abominate this damnable world. What is it—sham Virtues, sham Friendship, sham Everything; why, even its vices are sham. Bear it all, and sneer at it! Rise above it. With the Worms is Peace. All is Vanity, said the sage Jew, and every wise man since has said the same. And Destiny said:

A Beginning

"Sip thou of this cup, miserable mortal, thy journey is over, thy intolerable lassitude at an end." A Cynic is one who scrapes the Paint off the face of Truth. If only I could get away!

May 14th. Letter from Uncle Robert; still harping on my going away. And now he is mean enough to threaten L.S.D. as a trump card. "Some day they *shall* hear me! ! ! !"

May 15th. St. Barnabas's. Walked home from church with Fanny and could find positively nothing to say. My head keeps getting vacant.

May 17th. Caught in the rain. F. insisted on standing up under a chestnut tree. We were wet through. I have never seen any one so eager over mere trifles as she is. Her very fingers seem to speak. We were discussing what we would like to have been. "Ah," she said, "I would like to have been a gambler— every groat I had, and the lights would twirl—and there, a white mist of faces, and the hubbub of voices would fall away little in the distance—and my forehead all cold—and my heart go *so*. And then— O yes, that's it, that's it. To spend all and buy nothing. One vivid moment of wild viewless light —only once to fling away and forget poor narrow I and thou and they and all. . . . Look, the white sun comes reeling out and everything is on tip-toe, singing in the rain. It's just as it used to be with the rhymes in the old silly pigtail days. Verses on verses I'd scribble all about 'jetty hair' and 'eyes of fire' and 'dead sweet lovers'—I would sit down burning, my heart up here, in a very fine frenzy, and all would be mad ink and blurred brains, and in the midst of the scribble I would get up and come out and the wind would scatter all my poetry and blow me quite, quite sane again. And now—come! My voice is cracked."

We talked incessantly. And as luck would have it Mr. L. came out to meet her with wraps and umbrellas. He came stalking out of the distance over the dripping grass, staring into vacancy, his face as scarred and grey as an extinct volcano. But it looked uncommonly as if F. and I had met on the sly!

May 19th. I'm tired of trying to sympathize with people. They don't appreciate it, and you get nothing but ingratitude for your pains. We are all selfish at the roots.

May 20th. Met Fanny with G. M. Don't blame him, the puppy! and as for being jealous—! ! ! Derelict, derelict, derelict till the devil drops me a shot.

May 21st. Can do nothing. I am simply flotsam on the tide of life. I think it would be better to go away. I must work, work, work; that's the sovereign remedy. I am simply rotting as it is, so of course I get self-conscious and exaggerate things. Weak, erring Humanity has not the power to pierce the Mystery of things. We must toil blindly on. If only I had someone to confide in utterly, who would listen and never weary, and take me all in all! Headache. Went to bed early.

May 22nd. Can a leopard change his spots? Told Fanny after church that I had decided to take uncle's advice. She was extremely dejected. But I reasoned with her that it was all for the best, and pointed out that the heavier the present so much the easier would the future be. Poor child she has silly fancies of impending disaster. But it is best for her. God knows it is misery enough for me! Shall not mention my plans to Florence.

May 23rd. Wrote to uncle R.

May 25th. Woman's love is selfish, it will not bear analysis. Man's love is intellectual, and of the soul. Woman's is an instinct, a fleeting emotion. Henceforward I abjure ye all!

May 26th. Midnight. All is as I thought it would be. Every thing I do is rank and sour. I have proved myself an unutterable fool and blackguard, and that's enough. I really thought that I meant all I said. Why did I not keep to my vow and not go down? Why did I tell her about my going away? She seemed to fascinate me, her silence and her strange smile, and her sympathy. How could I have been so foolish; I see it all, the brightening moon and the boughs thick with blossom, and how she turned, pale and strange, and looked at me when I kissed her. She was almost beautiful with that half sorrowful smile. Her eyes haunt me. Her lips were burning hot. And to think that all this time she has seen through me. I wonder if she has guessed about Fanny. What would Fanny say?—and the others! My thoughts are in a black whirling chaos. I do not think I really understand love, but she must think I love her. And she made me feel so utterly mean and contemptible, when she refused to listen to me, as if I were a silly chattering child. And so calm and unmoved she was afterwards, like Mr. L. himself. I don't think he noticed anything, because she was perfectly calm, and her hands were like stones. But that woman Helen is as sharp as a ferret. I don't know which way to turn. What must she think of me, hypocrite and fool and traitor that I am! I must flee away into drudgery and solitude, and perhaps in the future the World may look in mercy on me—God knows I do not deserve mercy. There are moments in the life of a man, when the world is so bitter and himself so sour in his own mouth that even death is no hope, and Life one long interminable Woe.

(Letter from Nicholas to Florence)

My dear Florence,

I cannot reproach and despise myself sufficiently for my conduct of last evening. It was very ungentlemanly and unpardonable. The troubles and anxieties of the past few days have sorely unhinged me. I daresay you can imagine what difficulties must occur to a man on first setting out on his career. I am going on the 15th prox. You have been so kind to me and so hospitable that I feel I can never repay you, indeed I do; you have been infinitely more than a sister towards me, and I do not see why separation should make any difference to us. At least it will not to me. I cannot remember quite what I said. How was it that you had heard what you said you had? I trust you did not take cold; it was so very thought-less of me to keep you out in the garden. I hope you will take great care of yourself. I am not quite my-self at present so will write no more.

Believe me ever your sincere friend,

NICHOLAS.

P.S. Do you really like talking to me? It seemed like Destiny that our paths should cross. And indeed I hate myself and everything, and I think if you knew me you would see what I mean and forgive me.

May 27th. Am going on the 15th. Wrote to F. Fanny has no idea. She trusts in me implicitly. I swear never to undeceive her. I must not think of myself. Very busy all day making preparations. I think I am acting wisely—but Oh, the difference to me!

(Letter from Florence to Nicholas)

I *"understand"*. Indeed, I have indeed—forgotten all the sweet mad things you said to me and to the moon—was it not so? She was listening too—I saw her between the branches. Perhaps it is my shadows have whispered to me much about you—much that I could never have discovered for my poor self. You are going away to work, and I think it is much, much best for you; and if you knew what paths of glory I used to trace out for the child of my little black picture, and how I imagined my eagerness would help him on his way—just as his lonely com-

pany and his wistful child's eyes have helped me—
the very brightness of hope, you would not mind
my clapping my hands and urging you on. Yes, my
dear Nicholas, you must *work*, and I am glad to think
it is to my bleak haunted Cornwall you are going,
for there I can think of you where you are. And me
—why, here I shall be in my own familiar world of
solitude, just waiting. And if I do not forget you,
my own friend of the Springtime; and if sometimes
I turn back to the brief magic of the moon, you will
forgive me that. And forget my harshness, and my
awkward ways and tongue, remembering only that
I had kept faith with you these many, many years, and
am not ashamed. You just came into this world of
mine, as you were bound to come. And now, forget
me, and work on. May God keep thee, Nicholas.

F. L.

May 28th. Letter from Uncle R. enclosing cheque.

Also from F. How she despises me! Yet perhaps she
has taken me rightly. Who knows, if things had been
otherwise, if—but ifs make sour thinking. Work!
work!! work!!! that's the secret and goodbye to
sentiment. Talk is but braying.

June 13th. Went down to say goodbye. We walked
over the heath; but she was too tired to go far. And
we stayed by the Miller's Pool. It seemed another
world with its deep stars. We did not talk much.
Only once she stopped suddenly—as if she had forgotten something. "You see sometimes I cannot re-

member," she said, almost to herself. And we came back to the house. All the windows were dark. She looked very ill, as though she were troubled about something. I asked her to write to me. She looked at me, saying nothing. So we stood by the gates, and she turned away from me. "For you see it could not be words," she said. "O, it comes into my silence, and I cannot but hear. But you, perhaps you will write—and tell me about the place—and yourself. Where you are and what you are thinking and—oh, everything. Let me see your face once more—say nothing." So I took her hand and she told me to work and said that I must remember that of her. "Goodbye," she said, "just seven letters—goodbye, that is all." And she pushed back my hair and kissed me on the forehead. The gate swung to on its hinges. Its noise seemed to startle her, I fancy she cried out.

Then Helen opened the door and came out, and stared under the lamp towards me. Very soon Florence came running back. She stumbled and nearly fell on the path, but ran on coughing and laughing. "There," she said to me, panting after her running, "it is quite safe; I have brought you this." I see her now, looking through the bars of the iron gates at me, and before I could answer she was gone. And I heard Helen shooting the bolts of the front door as I remember watching Martha do in the winter evenings a grey eternity ago. So I was shut out.

It was the little picture she had given me. I took it out and looked at it by the dim suffused light of the moon. The house was quite dark and silent, so I thought it better not to go back, and thank her. I can't think why she gave me the picture. I thought she treasured it so. It was very mournful saying goodbye, but I feared she would have felt it more. So this is the end. It was all very strange, and my mind is confused and tired. Farewell to childishness. I am going solitary into exile and shall scribble no more. Day after day would be only the same whine; or sham and affectation which is worse. All diaries are. Thoughts spoken are thoughts belied. I think it higher and nobler for a man to plod patiently and silently on, through the impenetrable gloom; there may be light beyond. "Know thyself!" said the Ancient Sage. Every great man has been disciplined by solitude. I am a fool, and that confession is the herald of Wisdom.